# LYSISTRATA

by

# ARISTOPHANES

TRANSLATED BY
DOUGLASS PARKER

GENERAL EDITOR:
WILLIAM ARROWSMITH

A SIGNET CLASSIC

SIGNET CLASSIC
Published by New American Library, a division of
Penguin Group (USA) Inc., 375 Hudson Street,
New York, New York 10014, U.S.A.
Penguin Books Ltd, 80 Strand,
London WC2R 0RL, England
Penguin Books Australia Ltd, 250 Camberwell Road,
Camberwell, Victoria 3124, Australia
Penguin Books Canada Ltd, 10 Alcorn Avenue,
Toronto, Ontario, Canada M4V 3B2
Penguin Books (N.Z.) Ltd, Cnr Rosedale and Airborne Roads,
Albany, Auckland 1310, New Zealand

Penguin Books Ltd, Registered Offices:
80 Strand, London WC2R 0RL, England

Published by Signet Classic, an imprint of New American Library, a division
of Penguin Group (USA) Inc. Previously published in a Mentor edition.

First Signet Classic Printing, March 2001
10  9  8  7

Copyright © William Arrowsmith, 1964

All rights reserved

Library of Congress Catalog Card Number: 00-048230

Printed in the United States of America

BOOKS ARE AVAILABLE AT QUANTITY DISCOUNTS WHEN USED TO PROMOTE
PRODUCTS OR SERVICES. FOR INFORMATION PLEASE WRITE TO PREMIUM MAR-
KETING DIVISION, PENGUIN GROUP (USA) INC., 375 HUDSON STREET, NEW YORK,
NEW YORK 10014.

# CONTENTS

HAVERLY

CONIVGI CARISSIMAE

ΔΕΙΝΗΙ ΜΑΛΑΚΗΙ ΣΕΜΝΗΙ ΑΓΑΝΗΙ

SAEPE STVPEFACTVS SEMPER ADMIRATVS

HVNC LIBRVM INTERPRES

D. D. D. D. L. M.

# INTRODUCTION

## The Play

*Lysistrata* was first performed at Athens in the year 411 B.C., probably during the Lenaia. Of the achievement of that first production, we know nothing at all; of more recent developments, we are better informed.

Regular translation, frequent adaptation, persistent production, and occasional confiscation—these are the signs of success, making *Lysistrata* today's popular favorite among Aristophanes' surviving comedies. A not altogether joyous eminence. Even the most rabid advocate of the wide circulation of the classics-in-any-form must blanch slightly at the broadcast misconception that this play is a hoard of applied lubricity. Witness its latest American publication, bowdlerized-in-reverse, nestled near some choice gobbets from Frank Harris' autobiography in a slick and curious quarterly called *Eros*, now under indictment. If this be success, there is scant comfort in it.* What profit in outwearing time's ravages, only to win through to a general snigger? Both Aristophanes and his audience deserve better.

Happily, they do receive it. *Lysistrata* is Aristophanes' most popular play, not because it is his most obscene (it is

---

* Some, however: It is refreshing to conjecture what treatment Harris might have received from Aristophanes, who is by most standards quite orthodox in matters sexual. Compare his remarks on Ariphrades, especially at *Knights* 1280 ff.

not) nor his most prurient (he is never prurient), but because, to a present-day reader or viewer, it is his most com-
prehensible, capable of assimilation with the least violence
to preconceptions. Indeed, when we examine its preoccu-
pation with sex, the source of its notoriety, we find the treatment rather more soothing than shocking. Those facets of
the subject at which we, uneasy in our daintiness, are wont
to boggle, have nearly disappeared. Gone, almost, is the
homosexuality (now a clinical matter, hardly the object of
fun); gone the scatology (so uncomfortable in Monuments
of the Western Tradition). *Lysistrata* centers on what has
become for us the last refuge of genteel ribaldry—hetero-
sexual intercourse. If the presentation is more explicit than
we usually expect on a stage, we can still understand it and
conclude with the comforting generality that the Greeks
were, after all, just like us.

They were not, of course. They invested sex with little
transcendental significance, and nothing could have been
more foreign to them than the two most current misconstruc-
tions of *Lysistrata*—the mid-Victorian ("Brute Man
Saved from Himself by the Love of a Good Woman") and
the Reichian ("Happy Ganglia Make the Whole World
Kin"). *Lysistrata* concurs with Aristophanes' other briefs
for peace, *The Acharnians* and *The Peace*, in its basically
hedonistic approach: To the discomforts of war are op-
posed the joys of fulfilled desire. Admittedly, there have
been changes. The earlier plays interweave a triad of de-
sires—Wine, Food, and Sex; here, the first two members of
the triad are muted (though not dispensed with entirely),
and the third is explored to the full.

Predictably, this exploration of single theme rather than
cluster is preferred by certain critics to Aristophanes' normal practice in that it generates something curiously close
to the modern notion of a plot. Abetting this is the split
Chorus, which not only performs its normal function of a
control which limits and defines the main action, but paral-
lels that action with one of its own: gaffer loses crone,
gaffer gets crone. Put the parts together, let individual action be succeeded by the appropriate choral action, and the
result seems positively Well-Made. Though objection is

occasionally raised to a presumed lack of connection between the sex-strike and the seizure of the Akropolis, anyone who considers the terms in which that seizure is first defined—the old men's attack on the locked gates with logs they cannot lift, with fires they cannot light—will hardly be persuaded. And just as well. The connection is not just a structural ploy, but central to the play's meaning. The Akropolis, the heart of the city, is fused with the objects of desire, and its restoration is Love Achieved.

Love, not merely Sex—a vital distinction. If *Lysistrata* is not an exaltation of rut, neither is it a nihilistic satire which undercuts all human progress, all collective action, by cynically opposing to it the basic animality of the individual. Upsetting as it may seem to us, the heirs of a Puritan ethic, Aristophanes' hedonism is rarely anarchic. Certainly not here. The fundamental relationship is not blind sexual gratification, the force that drives the water through the rocks, any rocks, but love in its civic manifestation—the bond between husband and wife. Once this is established and identified with the City itself, Aristophanes can and does develop it into other areas. He can turn it around to show the wife and mother's proper share in the State, broaden it into a plea for Panhellenism, push it beyond sex entirely (in the split Choruses) to its irreducible residue. The neural itch is only the beginning; the goal is a united City and a unified Hellas at peace, the gift of Aphrodite. Significantly, the play ends with, not an orgy, but an invocation by Spartans and Athenians of the whole pantheon. *Eros* and *sophia*, sex and wisdom, join as the civilizing force of love.

Nobility of conception, of course, does not confer dignity of execution, and the basic ridiculousness of sex is rarely lost sight of. It is precisely this tension between intent and accomplishment, a tension all too visible in this most phallic of all comedies, that makes the play work. No character is exempt. Not even the heroine, whose somewhat prissy idealism cracks wide open for a moment at line 715 (all line numbers refer to original Greek text) in the inclusive cry *binêtiômen*—"we want to get laid." *Lysistrata* is a great play, not a so-so tract.

Still, there does exist a minority view. The play's technical excellences are unquestionable: tight formal unity, economy of movement, realism in characterizations, range of feeling. They are also rather un-Aristophanic excellences, and the specialist who prefers earlier, comparatively messy pieces may perhaps be forgiven. Certainly one point must be conceded him: At spots in *Lysistrata*, particularly during debates, Aristophanes' linguistic exuberance deserts him. I do not mean eloquence, but wit, the constant subterranean interplay of sound and sense which elsewhere makes poetry of argumentation. Whether this comes from haste, or from despair, or from the lack of balance which accompanies an overpowering desire to convince—the same lack that, to my mind, deforms the end of *The Clouds* —I cannot say. For whatever reason, it constitutes a blemish.

But a minor blemish on a major work, one tough-minded about sex, tough-minded about war. *Lysistrata*'s greatness ultimately resides in its sheer nerve, its thoroughgoing audacity in confronting, after twenty years of conflict, an Athens poised between external and internal disasters, between the annihilation of her Sicilian expeditionary force in 413 and the overthrow of her constitution in 411. With an astigmatism born of centuries, we are only too liable to misconstrue it, by refusing to see the heroine whole, by regarding the women's revolt as more possibility than fantasy, by giving way to sentimentality. But somehow we cannot do it much harm. Even when he writes like someone else, Aristophanes, servant of the Muses and Aphrodite, is Aristophanes still.

## Translation

In general, the principles of this translation remain those guiding my versions of *The Acharnians* and *The Wasps*. It is interpretive rather than literal. It cannot be used as a by-the-line crib, but aims at recreating in American English verse what I conceive to have been Aristophanes' essential strategies in Greek. To do this, fields of metaphor have often been changed, jokes added in compensation for jokes lost, useless proper names (primarily those of chorus members and supernumeraries) neglected. Not all of these changes have been indicated in the notes. Some particular points:

*Obscenity:* Though its workings may seem rococo at times, this version tries to be unblushing, and thus avoid the second greatest sin against Aristophanes, coyness. However, there is one area of compromise that must be justified: The language of the women has been slightly muted, not in the interest of propriety, but to make their characters viable to a modern audience. Lysistrata, for example, has more than a little of the *grande dame* about her, also an intriguing reluctance to refer directly to the relations between the sexes. When she must so refer, it is incongruous and funny—but a literal Englishing of *peous,* the last word in line 124 (here rendered, "Then here's the program: Total Abstinence from SEX!"), either by "penis" or by some curt Saxonism, would stretch the only available stereotype till it shattered, and reduced her assimilated social rank disastrously for the play.

*Proper Names:* Such is the power of tradition that the name of the heroine, and hence of the play, is here presented in its Latin form rather than in the straight transliteration from the Greek—"Lysistrate"—which would follow the normal practice for this series. But, in any case, the Latin rules for accent should hold, and the name be pronounced LySIStrata. Pronunciations of other principals: KleoNIky, MYRrhiny, LAMpito, KiNEEsias.

*Staging:* Those who hold that the Theater of Dionysos possessed, in the fifth century B.C., a stage raised above the level of the orchestra (i.e., of the Chorus' dancing area) will find ample proof of their contention in *Lysistrata*; those who maintain that such a raised stage was a fourth-century innovation will find it easy to discount such proof; I prefer to avoid the hassle altogether, though I lean to the fourth-century theory. But all the setting that is really needed is a building, center, with double doors, representing the entrance to the Akropolis, or Propylaia, on whose roof Lysistrata and her women can appear after the coup d'état. The prologue might profit slightly in the direction of literality by the presence of Lysistrata's house, right, and Kleonike's house, left. The first entrance of the Chorus of Men might gain (in the absence of parodoi) by a climbable hill; squeamish audiences might be helped over the Kinesias-Myrrhine encounter if it took place inside a Cave of Pan, Myrrhine appearing (rather than disappearing) briefly to obtain her props. All these are matters of individual taste, and affect the translation not at all. But one principle is at work throughout and must be observed: *Characters and Chorus do not normally mingle*. It is important to note certain applications of this general rule for this play: The Chorus of Women *at no time* enters the Akropolis, nor does it attack the Commissioner and his Skythians; these are the actions of different women, the younger women (most of them supers) who have joined in the oath toward the end of the Prologue. In my reading of the play, I see only one exception to the rule, and it is more apparent than actual: The abortive storming of the Akropolis by the united Chorus in the last scene, an attempt repulsed by the torch-bearing Commissioner.

# Text

I have worked most closely with Coulon's Budé text of 1928 and its immediate source, Wilamowitz' edition of 1927, supplementing them with little profit by the text of Cantarella (1956) and with great profit by those of Rogers (second edition, 1911) and Van Leeuwen (1903). But these worthies, singly or collectively, are not to be held responsible for certain features of the Greek underlying my translation. The characteristic weakness of the manuscripts of Aristophanes—their inability to answer with any certainty the recurrent question, "Who's talking?"—breaks out in its most virulent form in this most susceptible play; the translator, trying desperately to make dramatic sense of everything, must formulate his own replies. I have indicated in the notes my major departures from Coulon. Certain of these, particularly the continued presence of the Commissioner and Kinesias after their respective frustrations, may seem violent in the extreme. I can only state here that they are not arbitrary, but proceed from a reasoned examination of the problems involved.

Some minor solutions *are* arbitrary, of course, and scarcely susceptible of proof, as in line 122, where I have distributed between Kleonike and Myrrhine two words assigned by the manuscripts to Kleonike alone, for a purely pragmatic reason: it plays better that way. Again, my answer to the hackneyed query, "What woman delivers lines 447-448?"—to make Ismenia the Theban, heretofore mute, the speaker of two lines in Attic Greek—is an impossible solution to an impossible problem. Its only virtue is to bring in a previously introduced character without breaking the pattern—which, at that, is better than assigning the lines to the leader of the Women's Chorus.

This seeming disrespect for received writ has had its disturbing consequences, primarily an itch to fiddle further. The oath, for example: In the manuscripts, Lysistrata administers it (212 ff.) to the bibulous Kleonike as representative of the assembled women. In view of subsequent developments, might the responsions not better be made by Myrrhine, who will illustrate the practical applications of the oath? Or, to take the Commissioner, whose part I have already fattened considerably: Certain tricks of speech, coupled with his determination at 1011-1012 to make the necessary arrangements, suggest that he, rather than the Chorus (or Koryphaios), might be the official greeter of both the Spartan and the Athenian delegations, beginning the iambs at 1074 (p. 98, "Men of Sparta, I bid you welcome!"). But, though the will to refrain comes hard, I have, for the moment, stopped.

# Acknowledgments

My thanks go to the University of California, for typing grants; to Eleanore Stone, who fearlessly and impeccably typed and proofread the present version; to colleagues at Riverside, especially William Sharp, who enlightened me on drama; to colleagues in Washington, especially Kenneth Reckford, who enlightened me on Aristophanes. More than thanks to William Arrowsmith, who has taught me more about translation than I shall ever know; and to my wife, the dedicatee of this volume, who taught me about women without being a traitor to her sex.

DOUGLASS PARKER

# Characters of the Play

LYSISTRATA  
KLEONIKE } *Athenian women*  
MYRRHINE  
LAMPITO, *a Spartan woman*  
ISMENIA, *a Boiotian girl*  
KORINTHIAN GIRL  
POLICEWOMAN  
KORYPHAIOS OF THE MEN  
CHORUS OF OLD MEN *of Athens*  
KORYPHAIOS OF THE WOMEN  
CHORUS OF OLD WOMEN *of Athens*  
COMMISSIONER *of Public Safety*  
FOUR POLICEMEN  
KINESIAS, *Myrrhine's husband*  
CHILD *of Kinesias and Myrrhine*  
SLAVE  
SPARTAN HERALD  
SPARTAN AMBASSADOR  
FLUTE-PLAYER  
ATHENIAN WOMEN  
PELOPONNESIAN WOMEN  
PELOPONNESIAN MEN  
ATHENIAN MEN

SCENE: *A street in Athens. In the background, the Akropolis; center, its gateway, the Propylaia. The time is early morning.* Lysistrata is discovered alone, pacing back and forth in furious impatience.*

**LYSISTRATA**

*Women!*

Announce a debauch in honor of Bacchos,
a spree for Pan, some footling fertility fieldday,
and traffic stops—the streets are absolutely clogged
with frantic females banging on tambourines. No urging
for an orgy!

        But *today*—there's not one woman here.

*Enter Kleonike.*

Correction: one. Here comes my next door neighbor.
—Hello, Kleonike.*

**KLEONIKE**

        Hello to *you*, Lysistrata.
—But what's the fuss? Don't look so barbarous, baby;
knitted brows just aren't your style.

**LYSISTRATA**

        It doesn't
matter, Kleonike—I'm on fire right down to the bone.
I'm positively ashamed to be a woman—a member
of a sex which can't even live up to male slanders!
To hear our husbands talk, we're *sly*: deceitful,
always plotting, monsters of intrigue. . . .

**KLEONIKE**

*Proudly.*

        That's us!

**LYSISTRATA**

And so we agreed to meet today and plot
an intrigue that really deserves the name of monstrous . . .

and WHERE are the women?

Slyly asleep at home—
they won't get up for anything!

KLEONIKE

Relax, honey.
They'll be here. You know a woman's way is hard—
mainly the way out of the house: fuss over hubby,
wake the maid up, put the baby down, bathe him,
feed him . . .

LYSISTRATA

Trivia. They have more fundamental business to engage in.

KLEONIKE

Incidentally, Lysistrata, just why are
you calling this meeting? Nothing teeny, I trust?

LYSISTRATA

Immense.

KLEONIKE

Hmmm. And pressing?

LYSISTRATA

Unthinkably tense.

KLEONIKE

Then where IS everybody?

LYSISTRATA

Nothing like that. If it were,
we'd already be in session. Seconding motions.
—No, *this* came to hand some time ago. I've spent
my nights kneading it, mulling it, filing it down. . . .

KLEONIKE

Too bad. There can't be very much left.

**LYSISTRATA**

>                                   Only this:
> the hope and salvation of Hellas lies with the WOMEN!

**KLEONIKE**

Lies with the women? Now *there's* a last resort.

**LYSISTRATA**

It lies with us to decide affairs of state
and foreign policy.
>                    The Spartan Question: Peace
> or Extirpation?

**KLEONIKE**

>               How *fun!*
>                         I cast an Aye for Extirpation!

**LYSISTRATA**

The Utter Annihilation of every last Boiotian?

**KLEONIKE**

AYE!—I mean Nay. Clemency, please, for those
scrumptious eels.*

**LYSISTRATA**

>         And as for Athens . . . I'd rather not put
> the thought into words. Just fill in the blanks, if you will.
> —To the point: If we can meet and reach agreement
> here and now with the girls from Thebes and the
>     Peloponnese,
> we'll form an alliance and save the States of Greece!

**KLEONIKE**

Us? Be practical. Wisdom from women? There's nothing
cosmic about cosmetics—and Glamor i: our only talent.
All we can do is *sit*, primped and painted,
made up and dressed up,

*Getting carried away in spite of her argument.*

>                         ravishing in saffron wrappers,

peekaboo peignoirs, exquisite negligees, those chic,
expensive little slippers that come from the East . . .

**LYSISTRATA**

Exactly. You've hit it. I see our way to salvation
in just such ornamentation—in slippers and slips, rouge
and perfumes, negligees and decolletage. . . .

**KLEONIKE**

How so?

**LYSISTRATA**

So effectively that not one husband will take up his spear
against another . . .

**KLEONIKE**

Peachy!
I'll have that kimono
dyed . . .

**LYSISTRATA**

. . . or shoulder his shield . . .

**KLEONIKE**

. . . squeeze into that
daring negligee . . .

**LYSISTRATA**

. . . or unsheathe his sword!

**KLEONIKE**

. . . and buy those
slippers!

**LYSISTRATA**

Well, now. Don't you think the girls should be here?

**KLEONIKE**

*Be* here? Ages ago—they should have flown!

*She stops.*

But no. You'll find out. These are authentic Athenians:
no matter what they do, they do it late.

LYSISTRATA

But what about the out-of-town delegations? There isn't
a woman here from the Shore; none from Salamis . . .

KLEONIKE

*That's* quite a trip. They usually get on board
at sunup. Probably riding at anchor now.

LYSISTRATA

I thought the girls from Acharnai would be here first.
I'm especially counting on them. And they're not here.

KLEONIKE

I think Theogenes' wife is under way.
When I went by, she was hoisting her sandals . . .*

*Looking off right.*

But look!
Some of the girls are coming!

*Women enter from the right. Lysistrata looks off to the left
where more—a ragged lot—are straggling in.*

LYSISTRATA

And more over here!

KLEONIKE

Where did you find *that* group?

LYSISTRATA

They're from the outskirts.*

KLEONIKE

Well, that's something. If you haven't done anything
else, you've really ruffled up the outskirts.

*Myrrhine enters guiltily from the right.*

**MYRRHINE**

Oh, Lysistrata,
we aren't late, are we?
Well, *are* we?
Speak to me!

**LYSISTRATA**

What is it, Myrrhine? Do you want a medal for tardiness?
Honestly, such behavior, with so much at stake . . .

**MYRRHINE**

I'm sorry. I couldn't find my girdle in the dark.
And anyway, we're here now. So tell us all about it,
whatever it is.

**KLEONIKE**

No, wait a minute. Don't
begin just yet. Let's wait for those girls from Thebes
and the Peloponnese.

**LYSISTRATA**

Now *there* speaks the proper attitude.

*Lampito, a strapping Spartan woman, enters left, leading
a pretty Boiotian girl (Ismenia) and a huge, steatopygous
Korinthian.*

And here's our lovely Spartan.
He*ll*o, Lampito
dear.
Why darling, you're simply ravishing! Such
a blemishless complexion—so clean, so out-of-doors!
And will you look at that figure—the pink of perfection!

**KLEONIKE**

I'll bet you could strangle a bull.

**LAMPITO**

I calklate so.*
Hit's fitness whut done it, fitness and dancin'. You know
the step?

*Demonstrating.*

> Foot it out back'ards an' toe yore twitchet.

*The women crowd around Lampito.*

**KLEONIKE**

What unbelievably beautiful bosoms!

**LAMPITO**

> Shuckins,
whut fer you tweedlin' me up so? I feel like a heifer
come fair-time.

**LYSISTRATA**

*Turning to Ismenia.*

> And who is this young lady here?

**LAMPITO**

Her kin's purt-near the bluebloodiest folk in Thebes—
the First Fam'lies of Boiotia.

**LYSISTRATA**

*As they inspect Ismenia.*

> Ah, picturesque Boiotia:
her verdant meadows, her fruited plain . . .

**KLEONIKE**

*Peering more closely.*

> Her sunken
garden where no grass grows. A cultivated country.

**LYSISTRATA**

*Gaping at the gawking Korinthian.*

And who is *this*—er—little thing?

**LAMPITO**

> She hails
from over by Korinth, but her kinfolk's quality—mighty
big back there.

**KLEONIKE**

*On her tour of inspection.*

She's mighty big back *here.*

**LAMPITO**

The womenfolk's all assemblied. Who-all's notion
was this-hyer confabulation?

**LYSISTRATA**

Mine.

**LAMPITO**

Git on with the give-out.
I'm hankerin' to hear.

**MYRRHINE**

Me, too! I can't imagine
what could be so important. Tell us about it!

**LYSISTRATA**

Right away.
—But first, a question. It's not
an involved one. Answer yes or no.

*A pause.*

**MYRRHINE**

Well, ASK it!

**LYSISTRATA**

It concerns the fathers of your children—your husbands,
absent on active service. I know you all have men
abroad.
—Wouldn't you like to have them home?

**KLEONIKE**

My husband's been gone for the last five months! Way up
to Thrace, watchdogging military waste.* It's horrible!

MYRRHINE

Mine's been posted to Pylos for seven whole months!

LAMPITO

My man's no sooner rotated out of the line
than he's plugged back in. Hain't no discharge in this
war!

KLEONIKE

And lovers can't be had for love or money,
not even synthetics. Why, since those beastly Milesians
revolted and cut off the leather trade, that handy
do-it-yourself kit's *vanished* from the open market!

LYSISTRATA

If I can devise a scheme for ending the war,
I gather I have your support?

KLEONIKE

                        You can count on me!
If you need money, I'll pawn the shift off my back—

*Aside.*

and drink up the cash before the sun goes down.

MYRRHINE

Me, too! I'm ready to split myself right up
the middle like a mackerel, and give you half!

LAMPITO

Me, too! I'd climb Taygetos Mountain plumb
to the top to git the leastes' peek at Peace!

LYSISTRATA

Very well, I'll tell you. No reason to keep a secret.

*Importantly, as the women cluster around her.*

We can force our husbands to negotiate Peace,
Ladies, by exercising steadfast Self-Control—
By Total Abstinence . . .

*A pause.*

**KLEONIKE**

From WHAT?

**MYRRHINE**

Yes, what?

**LYSISTRATA**

You'll do it?

**KLEONIKE**

Of course we'll do it! We'd even *die!*

**LYSISTRATA**

Very well,
then here's the program:
Total Abstinence
from SEX!

*The cluster of women dissolves.*

—Why are you turning away? Where are you going?

*Moving among the women.*

—What's this? Such stricken expressions! Such gloomy
gestures!
—Why so pale?
—Whence these tears?
—What IS this?
Will you do it or won't you?
Cat got your tongue?

**KLEONIKE**

Afraid I can't make it. Sorry.
*On with the War!*

**MYRRHINE**

Me neither. Sorry.
*On with the War!*

**LYSISTRATA**

*This* from
my little mackerel? The girl who was ready, a minute
ago, to split herself right up the middle?

**KLEONIKE**

*Breaking in between Lysistrata and Myrrhine.*

Try something else. Try anything. If you say so,
I'm willing to walk through fire barefoot.
But not
to give up SEX—there's nothing like it, Lysistrata!

**LYSISTRATA**

*To Myrrhine.*

And you?

**MYRRHINE**

Me, too! I'll walk through fire.

**LYSISTRATA**

*Women!*
Utter sluts, the entire sex! Will-power,
nil. We're perfect raw material for Tragedy,
the stuff of heroic lays. "Go to bed with a god
and then get rid of the baby"—that sums us up!

*Turning to Lampito.*

—Oh, Spartan, be a dear. If *you* stick by me,
just you, we still may have a chance to win.
Give me your vote.

**LAMPITO**

Hit's right onsettlin' fer gals
to sleep all lonely-like, withouten no humpin'.
But I'm on yore side. We shore need Peace, too.

**LYSISTRATA**

You're a darling—the only woman here
worthy of the name!

**KLEONIKE**

       Well, just suppose we *did*,
as much as possible, abstain from . . . what you said,
you know—not that we *would*—could something like
that bring Peace any sooner?

**LYSISTRATA**

        Certainly. Here's how it works:
We'll paint, powder, and pluck ourselves to the last
detail, and stay inside, wearing those filmy
tunics that set off everything we *have*—

           and then
slink up to the men. They'll snap to attention, go
absolutely *mad* to love us—

       but we won't let them. We'll Abstain.
—I imagine they'll conclude a treaty rather quickly.

**LAMPITO**

*Nodding.*

Menelaos he tuck one squint at Helen's bubbies
all nekkid, and plumb throwed up.

*Pause for thought.*

        Throwed up his sword.

**KLEONIKE**

Suppose the men just leave us flat?

**LYSISTRATA**

        In that case,
we'll have to take things into our own hands.

**KLEONIKE**

There simply isn't any reasonable facsimile!
—Suppose they take us by force and drag us off
to the bedroom against our wills?

**LYSISTRATA**

        Hang on to the door.

**KLEONIKE**

Suppose they beat us?

**LYSISTRATA**

Give in—but be bad sports.
Be nasty about it—they don't enjoy these forced
affairs. So make them suffer.
Don't worry; they'll stop
soon enough. A married man wants harmony—
cooperation, not rape.

**KLEONIKE**

Well, I suppose so. . . .

*Looking from Lysistrata to Lampito.*

If *both* of you approve this, then so do we.

**LAMPITO**

Hain't worried over our menfolk none. We'll bring 'em
round to makin' a fair, straightfor'ard Peace
withouten no nonsense about it. But take this rackety
passel in Athens: I misdoubt no one could make 'em
give over thet blabber of theirn.

**LYSISTRATA**

They're our concern.
Don't worry. We'll bring them around.

**LAMPITO**

Not likely.
Not long as they got ships kin still sail straight,
an' thet fountain of money up thar in Athene's temple.*

**LYSISTRATA**

That point is quite well covered:
We're taking over
the Akropolis, including Athene's temple, today.
It's set: Our oldest women have their orders.
They're up there now, pretending to sacrifice, waiting

for us to reach an agreement. As soon as we do,
they seize the Akropolis.

LAMPITO

                    The way you put them thengs,
I swear I can't see how we kin possibly lose!

LYSISTRATA

Well, now that it's settled, Lampito, let's not lose
any time. Let's take the Oath to make this binding.

LAMPITO

Just trot out thet-thar Oath. We'll swear it.

LYSISTRATA

                          Excellent.
—Where's a policewoman?

*A huge girl, dressed as a Skythian archer (the Athenian
police) with bow and circular shield, lumbers up and gawks.*

                    —What are *you* looking for?

*Pointing to a spot in front of the women.*

Put your shield down here.

*The girl obeys.*

                    No, hollow *up!*

*The girl reverses the shield. Lysistrata looks about brightly.*

—Someone give me the entrails.

*A dubious silence.*

KLEONIKE

                    Lysistrata, what kind
of an Oath are we supposed to swear?

LYSISTRATA

                    The Standard.
Aischylos used it in a play, they say—the one where
you slaughter a sheep and swear on a shield.

**KLEONIKE**

Lysistrata,
you *do not* swear an Oath for *Peace* on a *shield!*

**LYSISTRATA**

What Oath do you want?

*Exasperated.*

Something bizarre and expensive?
A fancier victim—"Take one white horse and
disembowel"?

**KLEONIKE**

*White horse?* The symbolism's too obscure.*

**LYSISTRATA**

Then how
do we swear this oath?

**KLEONIKE**

Oh, *I* can tell you
*that,* if you'll let me.

First, we put an enormous
black cup right here—hollow up, of course.
Next, into the cup we slaughter a jar of Thasian
wine, and swear a mighty Oath that we won't . . .
dilute it with water.

**LAMPITO**

*To Kleonike.*

Let me corngratulate you—
that were the beatenes' Oath I ever heerd on!

**LYSISTRATA**

*Calling inside.*

Bring out a cup and a jug of wine!

*Two women emerge, the first staggering under the weight
of a huge black cup, the second even more burdened with
a tremendous wine jar. Kleonike addresses them.*

**KLEONIKE**

You darlings!
What a tremendous display of pottery!

*Fingering the cup.*

A girl
could get a glow just *holding* a cup like this!

*She grabs it away from the first woman, who exits.*

**LYSISTRATA**

*Taking the wine jar from the second serving woman (who exits), she barks at Kleonike.*

Put that down and help me butcher thi⸱ boar!

*Kleonike puts down the cup, over which she and Lysistrata together hold the jar of wine (the "boar"). Lysistrata prays.*

O Mistress Persuasion,
O Cup of Devotion,
Attend our invocation:
Accept this oblation,
Grant our petition,
Favor our mission.

*Lysistrata and Kleonike tip up the jar and pour the gurgling wine into the cup. Myrrhine, Lampito, and the others watch closely.*

**MYRRHINE**

Such an attractive shade of blood. And the spurt—
pure Art!

**LAMPITO**

Hit shore do smell mighty purty!

*Lysistrata and Kleonike put down the empty wine jar.*

**KLEONIKE**

Girls, let me be the first

*Launching herself at the cup.*

to take the Oath!

LYSISTRATA

*Hauling Kleonike back.*

You'll have to wait your turn like everyone else.
—Lampito, how do we manage with this mob?
                                        Cumbersome.
—Everyone place her right hand on the cup.

*The women surround the cup and obey.*

I need a spokeswoman. One of you to take
the Oath in behalf of the rest.

*The women edge away from Kleonike, who reluctantly finds
herself elected.*

                        The rite will conclude
with a General Pledge of Assent by all of you, thus
confirming the Oath. Understood?

*Nods from the women. Lysistrata addresses Kleonike.*

                        Repeat after me:

LYSISTRATA

**I will withhold all rights of access or entrance**

KLEONIKE

*I will withhold all rights of access or entrance*

LYSISTRATA

**From every husband, lover, or casual acquaintance**

KLEONIKE

*from every husband, lover, or casual acquaintance*

LYSISTRATA

**Who moves in my direction in erection.**

                        —Go on

KLEONIKE

*who m-moves in my direction in erection.*

                        Ohhhhh!
—Lysistrata, my knees are shaky. Maybe I'd better . . .

**LYSISTRATA**

**I will create, imperforate in cloistered chastity,**

KLEONIKE

*I will create, imperforate in cloistered chastity,*

**LYSISTRATA**

**A newer, more glamorous, supremely seductive me**

KLEONIKE

*a newer, more glamorous, supremely seductive me*

**LYSISTRATA**

**And fire my husband's desire with my molten allure—**

KLEONIKE

*and fire my husband's desire with my molten allure—*

**LYSISTRATA**

**But remain, to his panting advances, icily pure.**

KLEONIKE

*but remain, to his panting advances, icily pure.*

**LYSISTRATA**

**If he should force me to share the connubial couch,**

KLEONIKE

*If he should force me to share the connubial couch,*

**LYSISTRATA**

**I refuse to return his stroke with the teeniest twitch.**

KLEONIKE

*I refuse to return his stroke with the teeniest twitch.*

**LYSISTRATA**

**I will not lift my slippers to touch the thatch**

**KLEONIKE**

*I will not lift my slippers to touch the thatch*

**LYSISTRATA**

**Or submit sloping prone in a hangdog crouch.**

**KLEONIKE**

*or submit sloping prone in a hangdog crouch.*

**LYSISTRATA**

> **If I this oath maintain,**
> **may I drink this glorious wine.**

**KLEONIKE**

> *If I this oath maintain,*
> *may I drink this glorious wine.*

**LYSISTRATA**

> **But if I slip or falter,**
> **let me drink water.**

**KLEONIKE**

> *But if I slip or falter,*
> *let me drink water.*

**LYSISTRATA**

**—And now the General Pledge of Assent:**

**WOMEN**

                                    **A-MEN!**

**LYSISTRATA**

**Good. I'll dedicate the oblation.**

*She drinks deeply.*

**KLEONIKE**

                        **Not too much,**
**darling. You know how anxious we are to become**
**allies and friends.**

                    **Not to mention *staying* friends.**

*She pushes Lysistrata away and drinks. As the women take their turns at the cup, loud cries and alarums are heard offstage.*

LAMPITO

What-all's that bodacious ruckus?

LYSISTRATA

Just what I told you:
It means the women have taken the Akropolis. Athene's
Citadel is ours!
It's time for you to go,
Lampito, and set your affairs in order in Sparta.

*Indicating the other women in Lampito's group.*

Leave these girls here as hostages.

*Lampito exits left. Lysistrata turns to the others.*

Let's hurry inside
the Akropolis and help the others shoot the bolts.

KLEONIKE

Don't you think the men will send reinforcements
against us as soon as they can?

LYSISTRATA

So where's the worry?
The men can't burn their way in or frighten us out.
The Gates are ours—they're proof against fire and fear—
and they open only on our conditions.

KLEONIKE

Yes!
That's the spirit—let's deserve our reputations:

*As the women hurry off into the Akropolis.*

UP THE SLUTS!
WAY FOR THE OLD IMPREGNABLES!

*The door shuts behind the women, and the stage is empty.*

*A pause, and the Chorus of Men shuffles on from the left in two groups, led by their Koryphaios. They are incredibly aged Athenians; though they may acquire spryness later in the play, at this point they are sheer decrepitude. Their normally shaky progress is impeded by their burdens: each man not only staggers under a load of wood across his shoulders, but has his hands full as well—in one, an earthen pot containing fire (which is in constant danger of going out); in the other, a dried vinewood torch, not yet lit. Their progress toward the Akropolis is very slow.*

KORYPHAIOS OF MEN

*To the right guide of the First Semichorus, who is stumbling along in mild agony.*

> Forward, Swifty, keep 'em in step! Forget your shoulder.
> I know these logs are green and heavy—but duty, boy,
>    duty!

SWIFTY

*Somewhat inspired, he quavers into slow song to set a pace for his group.*

> I'm never surprised. At my age, life
> is just one damned thing after another.
> And yet, I never thought my wife
> was anything more than a home-grown bother.
>    But now, dadblast her,
>    she's a National Disaster!

FIRST SEMICHORUS OF MEN

> What a catastrophe—
>    *MATRIARCHY!*
> They've brought Athene's statue* to heel,
> they've put the Akropolis under a seal,
> they've copped the whole damned commonweal . . .
> What is there left for them to steal?

KORYPHAIOS OF MEN

*To the right guide of the Second Semichorus—a slower soul, if possible, than Swifty.*

Now, Chipper, speed's the word. The Akropolis, on the
   double!
Once we're there, we'll pile these logs around them, and
   convene
a circuit court for a truncated trial. Strictly impartial:
With a show of hands, we'll light a spark of justice under
every woman who brewed this scheme. We'll burn them
   all
on the first ballot—and the first to go is Ly . . .

*Pause for thought.*

is Ly . . .

*Remembering and pointing at a spot in the audience.*

is *Lykon's* wife—and there she is, right over there!*

CHIPPER

*Taking up the song again.*

> I won't be twitted, I won't be guyed,
> I'll teach these women not to trouble us!
> Kleomenes the Spartan tried
> expropriating our Akropolis*
> > some time ago—
> > ninety-five years or so—

SECOND SEMICHORUS OF MEN

> > but he suffered damaging losses
> > > when he ran across US!
> He breathed defiance—and more as well:
> No bath for six years—you could tell.
> We fished him out of the Citadel
> and quelled his spirit—but not his smell.

KORYPHAIOS OF MEN

That's how I took him. A savage siege:

Seventeen ranks

of shields were massed at that gate, with blanket infantry
   cover.
I slept like a baby.

So when mere women (who gall the gods

and make Euripides sick) try the same trick, should I
sit idly by?
                    Then demolish the monument I won at Marathon!

**FIRST SEMICHORUS OF MEN**

*Singly.*

> —The last lap of our journey!
> —I greet it with some dismay.
> —The danger doesn't deter me,
>                                   —but
> it's uphill
>           —all the way.
> —Please, somebody,
>                    —find a jackass
>            to drag these logs
>                           —to the top.
> —I ache to join the fracas,
>                         —but
>          my shoulder's aching
>                           —to stop.

**SWIFTY**

> Backward there's no turning.
> Upward and onward, men!
> And keep those firepots burning, or
> we make this trip again.

**CHORUS OF MEN**

*Blowing into their firepots, which promptly send forth
clouds of smoke.*

> With a puff (pfffff)....
> and a cough (hhhhhh)....
> The smoke! I'll choke! Turn it off!

**SECOND SEMICHORUS OF MEN**

*Singly.*

> —Damned embers.
>                —Should be muzzled.

—There oughta be a law.
—They jumped me
        —when I whistled
            —and then
they gnawed my eyeballs
        —raw.
—There's lava in my lashes.
—My lids are oxidized.
—My brows are braised.
        —These ashes are
volcanoes
    —in disguise.

**CHIPPER**

> This way, men. And remember,
> The Goddess needs our aid.
> So don't be stopped by cinders. Let's
> press on to the stockade!

**CHORUS OF MEN**

*Blowing again into their firepots, which erupt as before.*

> With a huff (hfffff). . . .
> and a chuff (chffff). . . .
> Drat that smoke. Enough is enough!

**KORYPHAIOS OF MEN**

*Signalling the Chorus, which has now tottered into position before the Akropolis gate, to stop, and peering into his firepot.*

Praise be to the gods, it's awake. There's fire in the old
    fire yet.
—Now the directions. See how they strike you:
                First, we deposit
these logs at the entrance and light our torches. Next, we
    crash
the gate. When that doesn't work, we request admission.
    Politely.
When *that* doesn't work, we burn the damned door
    down, and smoke

these women into submission,

That seem acceptable? Good.
Down with the load . . . ouch, that smoke! Sonofabitch!

*A horrible tangle results as the Chorus attempts to deposit the logs. The Koryphaios turns to the audience.*

Is there a general in the house? We have a logistical problem. . . .

*No answer. He shrugs.*

Same old story. Still at loggerheads over in Samos.*

*With great confusion, the logs are placed somehow.*

That's better. The pressure's off. I've got my backbone back.

*To his firepot.*

What, pot? You forgot your part in the plot?

Urge that smudge.
to be hot on the dot and scorch my torch.

Got it, pot?

*Praying.*

Queen Athene, let these strumpets
crumple before our attack.
Grant us victory, male supremacy . . .
and a testimonial plaque.

*The men plunge their torches into firepots and arrange themselves purposefully before the gate. Engaged in their preparations, they do not see the sudden entrance, from the right, of the Chorus of Women, led by their Koryphaios. These wear long cloaks and carry pitchers of water. They are very old—though not so old as the men—but quite spry. In their turn, they do not perceive the Chorus of Men.*

KORYPHAIOS OF WOMEN

*Stopping suddenly.*

What's this—soot? And smoke as well? I may be all wet, but this might mean fire. Things look dark, girls; we'll have to dash.

*They move ahead, at a considerably faster pace than the men.*

FIRST SEMICHORUS OF WOMEN

*Singly.*

> Speed! Celerity!      Save our sorority
> from arson. Combustion.      And heat exhaustion.
> Don't let our sisterhood      shrivel to blisterhood.
>    Fanned into slag by hoary typhoons.
>    By flatulent, nasty, gusty baboons.
>      We're late! Run!
>      The girls might be done!

*Tutte.*

> Filling my pitcher      was absolute torture:
> The fountains in town      are so *crowded* at dawn,
> glutted with masses      of the lower classes
> blatting and battering,      shoving, and shattering
> jugs. But I juggled      my burden, and wriggled
> away to extinguish      the igneous anguish
>
>    of neighbor, and sister, and daughter—
>      Here's Water!

SECOND SEMICHORUS OF WOMEN

*Singly.*

> Get wind of the news?      The gaffers are loose.
> The blowhards are off      with fuel enough
> to furnish a bathhouse.      But the finish is pathos:
>    They're scaling the heights with a horrid proposal.
>    They're threatening women with rubbish disposal!
>      How ghastly—how gauche!
>      burned up with the trash!

*Tutte.*

> Preserve me, Athene,      from gazing on any
> matron or maid      auto-da-fé'd.
> Cover with grace      these redeemers of Greece
> from battles, insanity,      Man's inhumanity.
> Gold-browed goddess,      hither to aid us!
> Fight as our ally,      join in our sally

against pyromaniac slaughter—
Haul Water!

**KORYPHAIOS OF WOMEN**

*Noticing for the first time the Chorus of Men, still busy at their firepots, she cuts off a member of her Chorus who seems about to continue the song.*

Hold it. What have we here? You don't catch true-blue patriots red-handed. These are authentic degenerates, male, taken *in flagrante.*

**KORYPHAIOS OF MEN**

Oops. Female troops. This could be upsetting. I didn't expect such a flood of reserves.

**KORYPHAIOS OF WOMEN**

Merely a spearhead. If our numbers stun you, watch that yellow streak spread. We represent just one percent of one percent of This Woman's Army.

**KORYPHAIOS OF MEN**

Never been confronted with such backtalk. Can't allow it. Somebody pick up a log and pulverize that brass.
Any volunteers?

*There are none among the male chorus.*

**KORYPHAIOS OF WOMEN**

Put down the pitchers, girls. If they start waving that lumber,
we don't want to be encumbered.

**KORYPHAIOS OF MEN**

Look, men, a few sharp jabs will stop that jawing. It never fails.
The poet Hipponax swears by it.*

*Still no volunteers. The Koryphaios of Women advances.*

KORYPHAIOS OF WOMEN

>               Then step right up. Have a jab at me.
Free shot.

KORYPHAIOS OF MEN

*Advancing reluctantly to meet her.*

>               Shut up! I'll peel your pelt. I'll pit your pod.

KORYPHAIOS OF WOMEN

The name is Stratyllis. I dare you to lay one finger on me.

KORYPHAIOS OF MEN

I'll lay on you with a fistful. Er—any specific threats?

KORYPHAIOS OF WOMEN

*Earnestly.*

I'll crop your lungs and reap your bowels, bite by bite,
and leave no balls on the body for other bitches to
gnaw.*

KORYPHAIOS OF MEN

*Retreating hurriedly.*

Can't beat Euripides for insight. And I quote:
>                         *No creature's found*
*so lost to shame as Woman.**
>                    Talk about realist playwrights!

KORYPHAIOS OF WOMEN

Up with the water, ladies. Pitchers at the ready, place!

KORYPHAIOS OF MEN

Why the water, you sink of iniquity? More sedition?

KORYPHAIOS OF WOMEN

Why the fire, you walking boneyard? Self-cremation?

KORYPHAIOS OF MEN

I brought this fire to ignite a pyre and fricassee your
friends.

**KORYPHAIOS OF WOMEN**

I brought this water to douse your pyre. Tit for tat.

**KORYPHAIOS OF MEN**

*You'll* douse my fire? Nonsense!

**KORYPHAIOS OF WOMEN**

You'll see, when the facts soak in.

**KORYPHAIOS OF MEN**

I have the torch right here. Perhaps I should barbecue
*you.*

**KORYPHAIOS OF WOMEN**

If you have any soap, I could give you a bath.

**KORYPHAIOS OF MEN**

A bath from those
polluted hands?

**KORYPHAIOS OF WOMEN**

Pure enough for a blushing young bridegroom.

**KORYPHAIOS OF MEN**

Enough of that insolent lip.

**KORYPHAIOS OF WOMEN**

It's merely freedom of speech.

**KORYPHAIOS OF MEN**

I'll stop that screeching!

**KORYPHAIOS OF WOMEN**

You're helpless outside of the jury-box.

**KORYPHAIOS OF MEN**

*Urging his men, torches at the ready, into a charge.*

Burn, fire, burn!

**KORYPHAIOS OF WOMEN**

*As the women empty their pitchers over the men.*

> And cauldron bubble.

**KORYPHAIOS OF MEN**

*Like his troops, soaked and routed.*

> Arrrgh!

**KORYPHAIOS OF WOMEN**

> Goodness.

What seems to be the trouble? Too hot?

**KORYPHAIOS OF MEN**

> Hot, hell! Stop it!

What do you think you're doing?

**KORYPHAIOS OF WOMEN**

> If you must know, I'm gardening.

Perhaps you'll bloom.

**KORYPHAIOS OF MEN**

> Perhaps I'll fall right off the vine!

I'm withered, frozen, shaking . . .

**KORYPHAIOS OF WOMEN**

> Of course. But, providentially,

you brought along your smudgepot.

> The sap should rise eventually.

*Shivering, the Chorus of Men retreats in utter defeat.*

*A Commissioner of Public Safety\* enters from the left, followed quite reluctantly by a squad of police—four Skythian archers. He surveys the situation with disapproval.*

**COMMISSIONER**

Fire, eh? Females again—spontaneous combustion
of lust. Suspected as much.

> Rubadubdubbing, incessant

incontinent keening for wine, damnable funeral

foofaraw for Adonis resounding from roof to roof—
heard it all before . . .

*Savagely, as the Koryphaios of Men tries to interpose a
remark.*

and WHERE?
The ASSEMBLY!
Recall, if you can, the debate on the Sicilian Question:
That bullbrained demagogue Demostratos (who will rot,
   I trust)
rose to propose a naval task force.
His wife,
writhing with religion on a handy roof, bleated
a dirge:
   "BEREFT! OH WOE OH WOE FOR ADONIS!"
And so of course Demostratos, taking his cue,
outblatted her:
   "A DRAFT! ENROLL THE WHOLE OF
ZAKYNTHOS!"
His wife, a smidgin stewed, renewed her yowling:
"OH GNASH YOUR TEETH AND BEAT YOUR
BREASTS FOR ADONIS!"
And so of course Demostratos (that god-detested blot,
   that foul-lunged son of an ulcer) gnashed tooth and nail
and voice, and bashed and rammed his program through.
And THERE is the Gift of Women:
MORAL CHAOS!

KORYPHAIOS OF MEN

Save your breath for actual felonies, Commissioner;
see what's happened to us! Insolence, insults,
these we pass over, but not lese-majesty:
We're flooded
with indignity from those bitches' pitchers—like a bunch
of weak-bladdered brats. Our cloaks are sopped. We'll
sue!

COMMISSIONER

Useless. Your suit won't hold water. Right's on their side.
For female depravity, gentlemen, WE stand guilty—

we, their teachers, preceptors of prurience, accomplices
before the fact of fornication. We sowed them in sexual
license, and now we reap rebellion.

> The proof?

Consider. Off we trip to the goldsmith's to leave
an order:

> "That bangle you fashioned last spring for my wife
> is sprung. She was thrashing around last night, and the
> prong
> popped out of the bracket. I'll be tied up all day—I'm
> boarding the ferry right now—but my wife'll be home.
> If you get the time, please stop by the house in a bit
> and see if you can't do something—anything—to fit
> a new prong into the bracket of her bangle."

> And bang.

Another one ups to a cobbler—young, but no apprentice,
full kit of tools, ready to give his awl—
and delivers this gem:

> "My wife's new sandals are tight.
> The cinch pinches her pinkie right where she's
> sensitive.
> Drop in at noon with something to stretch her cinch
> and give it a little play."

> And a cinch it is.

Such hanky-panky we have to thank for today's
Utter Anarchy: I, a Commissioner of Public
Safety, duly invested with extraordinary powers
to protect the State in the Present Emergency, have
secured
a source of timber to outfit our fleet and solve
the shortage of oarage. I need the money immediately . . .
and WOMEN, no less, have locked me out of the
Treasury!

*Pulling himself together.*

—Well, no profit in standing around.

*To one of the archers.*

> Bring
the crowbars. I'll jack these women back on their
pedestals!

—WELL, you slack-jawed jackass? What's the
attraction? Wipe that thirst off your face. I said *crow*bar,
not saloon!—All right, men, all together. Shove those
bars underneath the gate and HEAVE!

*Grabbing up a crowbar.*

I'll take this side.
And now let's root them out, men, ROOT them out.
One, Two . . .

*The gates to the Akropolis burst open suddenly, disclosing
Lysistrata. She is perfectly composed and bears a large
spindle. The Commissioner and the Police fall back in
consternation.*

LYSISTRATA

Why the moving equipment?
I'm quite well motivated, thank you, and here I am.
Frankly, you don't need crowbars nearly so much as
brains.

COMMISSIONER

Brains? O name of infamy! Where's a policeman?

*He grabs wildly for the First Archer and shoves him toward
Lysistrata.*

Arrest that woman!
Better tie her hands behind her.

LYSISTRATA

By Artemis, goddess of the hunt, if he lays a finger
on me, he'll rue the day he joined the force!

*She jabs the spindle viciously at the First Archer, who leaps,
terrified, back to his comrades.*

COMMISSIONER

What's this—retreat? Never! Take her on the flank.

*The First Archer hangs back. The Commissioner grabs the
Second Archer.*

—Help him.
              —Will the two of you kindly TIE HER UP?

*He shoves them toward Lysistrata. Kleonike, carrying a large chamber pot, springs out of the entrance and advances on the Second Archer.*

KLEONIKE

By Artemis, goddess of the dew,* if you so much
as touch her, I'll stomp the shit right out of you!

*The two Archers run back to their group.*

COMMISSIONER

*Shit?* Shameless! Where's another policeman?

*He grabs the Third Archer and propels him toward Kleonike.*

Handcuff *her* first. Can't stand a foul-mouthed female.

*Myrrhine, carrying a large, blazing lamp, appears at the entrance and advances on the Third Archer.*

MYRRHINE

By Artemis, bringer of light, if you lay a finger
on her, you won't be able to stop the swelling!

*The Third Archer dodges her swing and runs back to the group.*

COMMISSIONER

*Now* what? Where's an officer?

*Pushing the Fourth Archer toward Myrrhine.*

                         Apprehend that woman!
I'll see that *somebody* stays to take the blame!

*Ismenia the Boiotian, carrying a huge pair of pincers, appears at the entrance and advances on the Fourth Archer.*

ISMENIA*

By Artemis, goddess of Tauris, if you go near
that girl, I'll rip the hair right out of your head!

*The Fourth Archer retreats hurriedly.*

COMMISSIONER

What a colossal mess: Athens' Finest—
finished!

*Arranging the Archers.*

　　　　—Now, men, a little *esprit de corps.* Worsted
by women? Drubbed by drabs?
　　　　　　　　　　　　*Never!*
　　　　　　　　　　　　　　　　　Regroup,
reform that thin red line.
　　　　　　　　　　Ready?
　　　　　　　　　　　　　　CHARGE!

*He pushes them ahead of him.*

LYSISTRATA

I warn you. We have four battalions behind us—
full-armed combat infantrywomen, trained
from the cradle . . .

COMMISSIONER

　　　　　　　Disarm them, Officers! Go for the hands!

LYSISTRATA

*Calling inside the Akropolis.*

MOBILIZE THE RESERVES!

*A horde of women, armed with household articles, begins
to pour from the Akropolis.*

　　　　　　　　　　Onward, you ladies from hell!
Forward, you market militia, you battle-hardened
bargain hunters, old sales campaigners, grocery
grenadiers, veterans never bested by an overcharge!
You troops of the breadline, doughgirls—
　　　　　　　　　　　　INTO THE FRAY!
Show them no mercy!
　　　　　　　Push!
　　　　　　　　　Jostle!
　　　　　　　　　　　Shove!

Call them nasty names!
Don't be ladylike.

*The women charge and rout the Archers in short order.*

Fall back—don't strip the enemy! The day is ours!

*The women obey, and the Archers run off left. The Commissioner, dazed, is left muttering to himself.*

COMMISSIONER

Gross ineptitude. A sorry day for the Force.

LYSISTRATA

Of course. What did you expect? We're not slaves;
we're freeborn Women, and when we're scorned, we're
full of fury. Never Underestimate the Power of a Woman.

COMMISSIONER

Power? You mean Capacity. I should have remembered
the proverb: *The lower the tavern, the higher the
dudgeon.*

KORYPHAIOS OF MEN

Why cast your pearls before swine, Commissioner? I
    know you're a civil
servant, but don't overdo it. Have you forgotten the bath
they gave us—in public,
                            fully dressed,
                                        totally soapless?
Keep rational discourse for *people!*

*He aims a blow at the Koryphaios of Women, who dodges
and raises her pitcher.*

KORYPHAIOS OF WOMEN

                        I might point out that lifting
one's hand against a neighbor is scarcely civilized
behavior—and entails, for the lifter, a black eye.
                        I'm really peaceful by nature,

compulsively inoffensive—a perfect doll. My ideal is a
well-bred repose that doesn't even stir up dust . . .

*Swinging at the Koryphaios of Men with the pitcher.*

                                        unless some no-good lowlife
tries to rifle my hive and gets my dander up!

*The Koryphaios of Men backs hurriedly away, and the
Chorus of Men goes into a worried dance.*

CHORUS OF MEN

*Singly.*

> O Zeus, what's the use of this constant abuse?
> How do we deal with this female zoo?
> Is there no solution to Total Immersion?
> What can a poor man DO?

*Tutti.*

> Query the Adversary!
> Ferret out their story!
> What end did they have in view,
> to seize the city's sanctuary,
> snatch its legendary eyrie,
> snare an area so very
>     terribly taboo?

KORYPHAIOS OF MEN

*To the Commissioner.*

Scrutinize those women! Scour their depositions—assess
their rebuttals!
Masculine honor demands this affair be probed to the
bottom!

COMMISSIONER

*Turning to the women from the Akropolis.*

All right, you. Kindly inform me, dammit, in your own
words:
What possible object could you have had in blockading
the Treasury?

**LYSISTRATA**

We thought we'd deposit the money in escrow and
    withdraw you men
from the war.

**COMMISSIONER**

            The money's the cause of the war?

**LYSISTRATA**

                            And all our internal
disorders—the Body Politic's chronic bellyaches: What
causes Peisandros' frantic rantings, or the raucous cau-
cuses of the Friends of Oligarchy?* The chance for graft.
            But now, with the money up there,
they can't upset the City's equilibrium—or lower its
balance.

**COMMISSIONER**

And what's your next step?

**LYSISTRATA**

            Stupid question. We'll budget the money.

**COMMISSIONER**

*You'll budget the money?*

**LYSISTRATA**

            Why should you find that so shocking?
We budget the household accounts, and you don't object
at all.

**COMMISSIONER**

That's different.

**LYSISTRATA**

            Different? How?

**COMMISSIONER**

            The War Effort needs this money!

**LYSISTRATA**

Who needs the War Effort?

**COMMISSIONER**

Every patriot who pulses to save
all that Athens holds near and dear . . .

**LYSISTRATA**

Oh, *that*. Don't worry.
We'll save you.

**COMMISSIONER**

*You* will save us?

**LYSISTRATA**

Who else?

**COMMISSIONER**

But this is unscrupulous!

**LYSISTRATA**

We'll save you. You can't deter us.

**COMMISSIONER**

Scurrilous!

**LYSISTRATA**

You seem disturbed.
This makes it difficult. But, still—we'll save you.

**COMMISSIONER**

Doubtless illegal!

**LYSISTRATA**

We deem it a duty. For friendship's sake.

**COMMISSIONER**

Well, forsake this friend:
I DO NOT WANT TO BE SAVED, DAMMIT!

**LYSISTRATA**

All the more reason.
It's not only Sparta; now we'll have to save you from
you.

COMMISSIONER

Might I ask where you women conceived this concern about War and Peace?

LYSISTRATA

*Loftily.*

We shall explain.

COMMISSIONER

*Making a fist.*

Hurry up, and you won't get hurt.

LYSISTRATA

Then *listen*. And do try to keep your hands to yourself.

COMMISSIONER

*Moving threateningly toward her.*

I can't. Righteous anger forbids restraint, and decrees . . .

KLEONIKE

*Brandishing her chamber pot.*

Multiple fractures?

COMMISSIONER

*Retreating.*

Keep those croaks for yourself, you old crow!

*To Lysistrata.*

All right, lady, I'm ready. Speak.

LYSISTRATA

I shall proceed:

When the War began, like the prudent, dutiful wives that we are, we tolerated you men, and endured your actions in silence. (Small wonder—

you wouldn't let us say boo.)

> You were not precisely the answer
to a matron's prayer—we knew you too well, and found
out more.

Too many times, as we sat in the house, we'd hear that
you'd done it again—manhandled another affair of
state with your usual staggering incompetence. Then,
masking our worry with a nervous laugh,
we'd ask you, brightly, "How was the Assembly today,
dear? Anything
in the minutes about Peace?" And my husband would
give his stock reply.
"What's that to you? Shut up!" And I did.

KLEONIKE

*Proudly.*

> *I* never shut up!

COMMISSIONER

I trust you were shut up. Soundly.

LYSISTRATA

> Regardless, *I* shut up.
And then we'd learn that you'd passed another decree,
fouler than the first, and we'd ask again: "Darling, how
*did* you manage anything so idiotic?" And my
husband, with his customary glare, would tell me to spin
my thread, or else get a clout on the head.
And of course he'd quote from Homer:
> *Yᵉ menne must husband yᵉ warre.**

COMMISSIONER

Apt and irrefutably right.

LYSISTRATA

> *Right*, you miserable misfit?
To keep us from giving advice while you fumbled the
City away in the Senate? Right, indeed!
> But this time was really too much:

Wherever we went, we'd hear you engaged in the same
 conversation:
"What Athens needs is a Man."*
                "But there isn't a Man in the country."
"You can say that again."
                There was obviously no time to lose.
We women met in immediate convention and passed a
unanimous resolution: To work in concert for safety and
Peace in Greece. We have valuable advice to impart,
and if you can possibly deign to emulate our silence,
and take your turn as audience, we'll rectify you—
we'll straighten you out and set you right.

**COMMISSIONER**

*You'll* set *us* right? You go too far. I cannot permit
such a statement to . . .

**LYSISTRATA**

                Shush.

**COMMISSIONER**

                I categorically decline to shush
for some confounded woman, who wears—as a constant
reminder of congenital inferiority, an injunction to
public silence—a veil!
Death before such dishonor!

**LYSISTRATA**

*Removing her veil.*

                If that's the only obstacle . . .
        I feel you need a new panache,
        so take the veil, my dear Commis-
            sioner, and drape it thus—
                and SHUSH!

*As she winds the veil around the startled Commissioner's
head, Kleonikē and Myrrhinē, with carding-comb and wool-
basket, rush forward and assist in transforming him into a
woman.*

**KLEONIKE**

> Accept, I pray, this humble comb.

**MYRRHINE**

> Receive this basket of fleece as well.

**LYSISTRATA**

> Hike up your skirts, and card your wool,
> and gnaw your beans—and stay at home!
> While we rewrite Homer:
> *Y^e WOMEN must WIVE y^e warre!*

*To the Chorus of Women, as the Commissioner struggles to remove his new outfit.*

> Women, weaker vessels, arise!
>                         Put down your pitchers.
> It's our turn, now. Let's supply our friends with some
> moral support.

*The Chorus of Women dances to the same tune as the Men, but with much more confidence.*

**CHORUS OF WOMEN**

*Singly.*

> Oh, yes! I'll dance to bless their success.
> Fatigue won't weaken my will. Or my knees.
> I'm ready to join in any jeopardy.
>     with girls as good as *these*!

*Tutte.*

> A tally of their talents
> convinces me they're giants
> of excellence. To commence:
> there's Beauty, Duty, Prudence, Science,
> Self-Reliance, Compliance, Defiance,
> and Love of Athens in balanced alliance
>     with Common Sense!

**KORYPHAIOS OF WOMEN**

*To the women from the Akropolis.*

Autochthonous daughters of Attika, sprung from the
soil that bore your mothers, the spiniest, spikiest
nettles known to man, prove your mettle and attack!
Now is no time to dilute your anger. You're
running ahead of the wind!

**LYSISTRATA**

We'll wait for the wind
from heaven. The gentle breath of Love and his Kyprian
mother will imbue our bodies with desire, and raise a
storm to tense and tauten these blasted men until they
crack. And soon we'll be on every tongue in
Greece—the *Pacifiers.*\*

**COMMISSIONER**

That's quite
a mouthful. How will you win it?

**LYSISTRATA**

First, we intend to withdraw
that crazy Army of Occupation from the downtown
shopping section.

**KLEONIKE**

Aphrodite be praised!

**LYSISTRATA**

The pottery shop and the grocery stall
are overstocked with soldiers, clanking around like
those maniac Korybants,
armed to the teeth for a battle.

**COMMISSIONER**

A Hero is Always Prepared!

**LYSISTRATA**

I suppose he is. But it does look silly to shop for sardines
from behind a shield.

**KLEONIKE**

I'll second that. I saw
a cavalry captain buy vegetable soup on horseback. He
carried the whole mess home in his helmet.

And then that fellow from Thrace,
shaking his buckler and spear—a menace straight from
the stage.
The saleslady was stiff with fright. He was hogging her
ripe figs—free.

**COMMISSIONER**

I admit, for the moment, that Hellas' affairs are in one
hell of a snarl. But how can you set them straight?

**LYSISTRATA**

Simplicity itself.

**COMMISSIONER**

Pray demonstrate.

**LYSISTRATA**

It's rather like yarn. When a hank's in a tangle,
we lift it—*so*—and work out the snarls by winding it up
on spindles, now this way, now that way.

That's how we'll wind up the War,
if allowed: We'll work out the snarls by sending Special
Commissions—
back and forth, now this way, now that way—to ravel
these tense international kinks.

**COMMISSIONER**

I lost your thread, but I know there's a hitch.
Spruce up the world's disasters with spindles—typically
woolly female logic.

**LYSISTRATA**

If *you* had a scrap of logic, you'd adopt
our wool as a master plan for Athens.

COMMISSIONER

What course of action
does the wool advise?

LYSISTRATA

Consider the City as fleece, recently
shorn. The first step is Cleansing: Scrub it in a public
bath, and remove all corruption, offal, and sheepdip.
Next, to the couch
for Scutching and Plucking: Cudgel the leeches and
similar vermin loose with a club, then pick the prickles
and cockleburs out. As for the clots—those lumps
that clump and cluster in knots and snarls to snag
important posts*—you comb these out,
twist off their heads, and discard.
Next, to raise the City's
nap, you card the citizens together in a single basket
of common weal and general welfare. Fold in our loyal
Resident Aliens, all Foreigners of proven and tested
friendship, and any Disenfranchised Debtors. Combine
these closely with the rest.
Lastly, cull the colonies settled by our own people:
these are nothing but flocks of wool from the City's
fleece, scattered throughout the world. So gather home
these far-flung flocks, amalgamate them with the
others.
Then, drawing this blend
of stable fibers into one fine staple, you spin a mighty
bobbin of yarn—and weave, without bias or seam, a
cloak to clothe the City of Athens!

COMMISSIONER

This is too much! The City's
died in the wool, worsted by the distaff side—by women
who bore no share in the War. . . .

LYSISTRATA

None, you hopeless hypocrite?
The quota we bear is double. First, we delivered our
sons to fill out the front lines in Sicily . . .

COMMISSIONER

>              Don't tax me with that memory.

LYSISTRATA

Next, the best years of our lives were levied. Top-level
strategy attached our joy, and we sleep alone.

>                                But it's not the matrons
like us who matter. I mourn for the virgins, bedded in
single blessedness, with nothing to do but grow old.

COMMISSIONER

>                           Men *have* been known
to age, as well as women.

LYSISTRATA

>                    No, not as well as—better.
A man, an absolute antique, comes back from the war,
     and he's barely
doddered into town before he's married the veriest
     nymphet.
But a woman's season is brief; it slips, and she'll have
no husband, but sit out her life groping at omens—
     and finding no men.

COMMISSIONER

Lamentable state of affairs. Perhaps we can rectify
     matters:

*To the audience.**

TO EVERY MAN JACK, A CHALLENGE:
>                                ARISE!
Provided you can . . .

LYSISTRATA

Instead, Commissioner, why not simply curl up and *die?*
>          Just buy a coffin; here's the place.

*Banging him on the head with her spindle.**

>              I'll knead you a cake for the wake—and *these*

*Winding the threads from the spindle around him.*

> make excellent wreaths. So Rest In Peace.

**KLEONIKE**

*Emptying the chamber pot over him.*

> Accept these tokens of deepest grief.

**MYRRHINE**

*Breaking her lamp over his head.*

> A final garland for the dear deceased.

**LYSISTRÁTA**

> May I supply any last request?
> Then run along. You're due at the wharf:
> Charon's anxious to sail—
> you're holding up the boat for Hell!

**COMMISSIONER**

This is monstrous—maltreatment of a public official—
maltreatment of ME!
> I must repair directly
to the Board of Commissioners, and present my
colleagues concrete evidence of the sorry specifics of
this shocking attack!

*He staggers off left. Lysistrata calls after him.*

**LYSISTRATA**

You won't haul us into court on a charge of neglecting
the dead, will you? (How like a man to insist
on his rights—even his last ones.) Two days between
death and funeral, that's the rule.
> Come back here early
day after tomorrow, Commissioner:
> We'll lay you out.

*Lysistrata and her women re-enter the Akropolis. The Koryphaios of Men advances to address the audience.*

**KORYPHAIOS OF MEN**

Wake up, Athenians! Preserve your freedom—the time
is Now!

*To the Chorus of Men.*

Strip for action, men. Let's cope with the current mess.

*The men put off their long mantles, disclosing short tunics
underneath, and advance toward the audience.*

**CHORUS OF MEN**

This trouble may be terminal; it has a loaded odor,
    an ominous aroma of constitutional rot.
My nose gives a prognosis of radical disorder—
    it's just the first installment of an absolutist plot!
        The Spartans are behind it:
        they must have masterminded
some morbid local contacts (engineered by Kleisthenes).
        Predictably infected,
        these women straightway acted
to commandeer the City's cash. They're feverish to freeze
        my be-all,
        my end-all . . .
        my *payroll!**

**KORYPHAIOS OF MEN**

The symptoms are clear. Our birthright's already
    nibbled. And oh, so
daintily: WOMEN ticking off troops* for improper
    etiquette.
WOMEN propounding their featherweight views on the
    fashionable use
and abuse of the shield. And (if any more proof were
    needed) WOMEN
nagging us to trust the Nice Spartan, and put our heads
in his toothy maw—to make a dessert and call it Peace.
They've woven the City a seamless shroud, bedecked
    with the legend
DICTATORSHIP.
                But I won't be hemmed in. I'll use

their weapon against them, and uphold the right
  by sneakiness.
                   With knyf under cloke,
gauntlet in glove, sword in olivebranch,

*Slipping slowly toward the Koryphaios of Women.*

                         I'll take up my post
in Statuary Row, beside our honored National Heroes,
the natural foes of tyranny: Harmodios,
                               Aristogeiton,
                                 and Me.*

*Next to her.*

Striking an epic pose, so, with the full approval
of the immortal gods,
                    I'll bash this loathesome hag in the jaw!

*He does, and runs cackling back to the Men. She shakes
a fist after him.*

KORYPHAIOS OF WOMEN

Mama won't know her little boy when he gets home!

*To the Women, who are eager to launch a full-scale attack.*

Let's not be hasty, fellow . . . hags. Cloaks off first.

*The Women remove their mantles, disclosing tunics very
like those of the Men, and advance toward the audience.*

CHORUS OF WOMEN

We'll address you, citizens, in beneficial, candid,
  patriotic accents, as our breeding says we must,
since, from the age of seven, Athens graced me with a
  splendid string of civic triumphs to signalize her
    trust:
        I was Relic-Girl quite early,
        then advanced to Maid of Barley;
in Artemis' "Pageant of the Bear" I played the lead.
        To cap this proud progression,*
        I led the whole procession
at Athene's Celebration, certified and pedigreed

> —that cachet
> so distingué—
> a *Lady!*

**KORYPHAIOS OF WOMEN**

*To the audience.*

I trust this establishes my qualifications. I may, I take it,
address the City to its profit? Thank you.

I admit to being a woman—
but don't sell my contribution short on that account.
It's better than the present panic. And my word is as
good as my bond, because I hold stock in Athens—
stock I paid for in sons.

*To the Chorus of Men.*

—But you, you doddering bankrupts, where are your
shares in the State?

*Slipping slowly toward the Koryphaios of Men.*

Your grandfathers willed you the Mutual Funds from
    the Persian War*—
and where are they?

*Nearer.*

You dipped into capital, then lost interest . . .
and now a pool of your assets won't fill a hole in the
    ground.
All that remains is one last potential killing—Athens.
Is there any rebuttal?

*The Koryphaios of Men gestures menacingly. She ducks
down, as if to ward off a blow, and removes a slipper.*

Force is a footling resort. I'll take
my very sensible shoe, and paste you in the jaw!

*She does so, and runs back to the women.*

**CHORUS OF MEN**

Their native respect for our manhood is small,
and keeps getting smaller. Let's bottle their gall.
The man who won't battle has no balls at all!

**KORYPHAIOS OF MEN**

All right, men, skin out of the skivvies. Let's give them
a whiff of Man, full strength. No point in muffling
the essential Us.

*The men remove their tunics.*

**CHORUS OF MEN**

> A century back, we soared to the Heights*
>     and beat down Tyranny there.
> Now's the time to shed our moults
>     and fledge our wings once more,
> ω rise to the skies in our reborn force,
>     and beat back Tyranny here!

**KORYPHAIOS OF MEN**

No fancy grappling with these grannies; straightforward
    strength. The tiniest
toehold, and those nimble, fiddling fingers will have their
foot in the door, and we're done for.

>               *No amount of know-how can lick
> a woman's knack.*

>               They'll want to build ships . . . next thing we
>     know,
we're all at sea, fending off female boarding parties.
(Artemisia fought us at Salamis. Tell me, has anyone
caught her yet?)

>       But we're *really* sunk if they take up horses. Scratch
the Cavalry:

>               A woman is an easy rider with a natural seat.
Take her over the jumps bareback, and she'll never slip
her mount. (That's how the Amazons nearly took
    Athens. On horseback.
Check on Mikon's mural down in the Stoa.)

>                               Anyway,
the solution is obvious. Put every woman in her place—
stick her in the stocks.

>       To do this, first snare your woman around the neck.

*He attempts to demonstrate on the Koryphaios of Women.
After a brief tussle, she works loose and chases him back
to the Men.*

CHORUS OF WOMEN

> The beast in me's eager and fit for a brawl.
> Just rile me a bit and she'll kick down the wall.
> You'll bawl to your friends that you've no balls at all.

KORYPHAIOS OF WOMEN

All right, ladies, strip for action. Let's give them a whiff of *Femme Enragée*—piercing and pungent, but not at all tart.

*The women remove their tunics.*

CHORUS OF WOMEN

> We're angry. The brainless bird who tangles
> with *us* has gummed his last mush.
> In fact, the coot who even heckles
> is being daringly rash.
> So look to your nests, you reclaimed eagles—
> whatever you lay, we'll squash!

KORYPHAIOS OF WOMEN

Frankly, you don't faze me. *With* me, I have my
   friends—
Lampito from Sparta; that genteel girl from Thebes,
   Ismenia—
committed to me forever. *Against* me, *you*—permanently
out of commission. So do your damnedest.
                                           Pass a law.
Pass seven. Continue the winning ways that have made
your name a short and ugly household word.
                                           Like yesterday:
I was giving a little party, nothing fussy, to honor
the goddess Hekate. Simply to please my daughters,
I'd invited a sweet little thing from the neighborhood—
   flawless pedigree, perfect
taste, a credit to any gathering—a Boiotian eel.
But she had to decline. Couldn't pass the border. You'd
   passed a law.
Not that you care for my party. You'll overwork your
   right of passage

till your august body is overturned,
>                     and you break your silly neck!

*She deftly grabs the Koryphaios of Men by the ankle and
upsets him. He scuttles back to the Men, who retire in
confusion.*

*Lysistrata emerges from the citadel, obviously distraught.*

**KORYPHAIOS OF WOMEN**

*Mock-tragic.*

> *Mistress, queen of this our subtle scheme,
> why burst you from the hall with brangled brow?*

**LYSISTRATA**

> *Oh, wickedness of woman! The female mind
> does sap my soul and set my wits a-totter.*

**KORYPHAIOS OF WOMEN**

*What drear accents are these?*

**LYSISTRATA**

>                     *The merest truth.*

**KORYPHAIOS OF WOMEN**

*Be nothing loath to tell the tale to friends.*

**LYSISTRATA**

*'Twere shame to utter, pain to hold unsaid.*

**KORYPHAIOS OF WOMEN**

*Hide not from me affliction which we share.*

**LYSISTRATA**

*In briefest compass,*
Dropping the paratragedy.

>           we want to get laid.

**KORYPHAIOS OF WOMEN**

>                     By Zeus!

**LYSISTRATA**

No, no, not HIM!
                    Well, that's the way things are.
I've lost my grip on the girls—they're mad for men!
But sly—they slip out in droves.
                    A minute ago,
I caught one scooping out the little hole
that breaks through just below Pan's grotto.*
                    One
had jerry-rigged some block-and-tackle business
and was wriggling away on a rope.
                    Another just flat
deserted.
      Last night I spied one mounting a sparrow,
all set to take off for the nearest bawdyhouse. I hauled
her back by the hair.
                    And excuses, pretexts for overnight
passes? I've heard them all.
                    Here comes one. Watch.

*To the First Woman, as she runs out of the Akropolis.*

—You, there! What's your hurry?

**FIRST WOMAN**

                    I have to get home.
I've got all this lovely Milesian wool in the house,
and the moths will simply batter it to bits!

**LYSISTRATA**

                    I'll bet.

Get back inside.

**FIRST WOMAN**

      I swear I'll hurry right back!
—Just time enough to spread it out on the couch?

**LYSISTRATA**

Your wool will stay unspread. And you'll stay here.

**FIRST WOMAN**

Do I have to let my piecework *rot?*

**LYSISTRATA**

Possibly.

*The Second Woman runs on.*

**SECOND WOMAN**

Oh dear, oh goodness, what shall I do—my flax!
I left and forgot to peel it!

**LYSISTRATA**

Another one.
She suffers from unpeeled flax.
—Get back inside!

**SECOND WOMAN**

I'll be right back. I just have to pluck the fibers.

**LYSISTRATA**

No. No plucking. You start it, and everyone else
will want to go and do their plucking, too.

*The Third Woman, swelling conspicuously, hurries on,
praying loudly.*

**THIRD WOMAN**

*O Goddess of Childbirth, grant that I not deliver
until I get me from out this sacred precinct!*

**LYSISTRATA**

What sort of nonsense is *this?*

**THIRD WOMAN**

I'm due—any second!

**LYSISTRATA**

You weren't pregnant yesterday.

**THIRD WOMAN**

Today I am—

a miracle!
Let me go home for a midwife, *please!*
I may not make it!

**LYSISTRATA**

*Restraining her.*

You can do better than that.

*Tapping the woman's stomach and receiving a metallic clang.*

What's this? It's hard.

**THIRD WOMAN**

I'm going to have a boy.

**LYSISTRATA**

Not unless he's made of bronze. Let's see.

*She throws open the Third Woman's cloak, exposing a huge bronze helmet.*

Of all the brazen . . . You've stolen the helmet from
Athene's statue! Pregnant, indeed!

**THIRD WOMAN**

I am *so* pregnant!

**LYSISTRATA**

Then why the helmet?

**THIRD WOMAN**

I thought my time might come
while I was still on forbidden ground. If it did,
I could climb inside Athene's helmet and have
my baby there.
The pigeons do it all the time.

**LYSISTRATA**

Nothing but excuses!

*Taking the helmet.*

> *This* is your baby. I'm afraid
you'll have to stay until we give it a name.

**THIRD WOMAN**

But the Akropolis is *awful*. I can't even sleep! I saw
the snake that guards the temple.

**LYSISTRATA**

> That snake's a fabrication.*

**THIRD WOMAN**

I don't care *what* kind it is—I'm *scared!*

*The other women, who have emerged from the citadel,
crowd around.*

**KLEONIKE**

And those goddamned holy owls; All night long,
*tu-wit, tu-wu*—they're hooting me into my grave!

**LYSISTRATA**

Darlings, let's call a halt to this hocus-pocus.
You miss your men—now isn't that the trouble?

*Shamefaced nods from the group.*

> Don't you think they miss you just as much?
I can assure you, their nights are every bit
as hard as yours. So be good girls; endure!
Persist a few days more, and Victory is ours.
It's fated: a current prophecy declares that the men
will go down to defeat before us, provided that *we*
maintain a United Front.

*Producing a scroll.*

> I happen to have
a copy of the prophecy.

KLEONIKE

Read it!

LYSISTRATA

Silence, *please*:

*Reading from the scroll.*

But when the swallows, in flight from the
    hoopoes, have flocked to a hole
on high, and stoutly eschew their
    accustomed perch on the pole,
yea, then shall Thunderer Zeus to
    their suff'ring establish a stop,
by making the lower the upper . . .

KLEONIKE

Then *we'll* be lying on top?

LYSISTRATA

But should these swallows, indulging their
    lust for the perch, lose heart,
dissolve their flocks in winged dissension,
    and singly depart
the sacred stronghold, breaking the
    bands that bind them together—
then know them as lewd, the pervertedest
    birds that ever wore feather.

KLEONIKE

There's nothing obscure about *that* oracle. Ye gods!

LYSISTRATA

Sorely beset as we are, we must not flag
or falter. So back to the citadel!

*As the women troop inside.*

And if we fail
that oracle, darlings, our image is absolutely *mud!*

*She follows them in. A pause, and the Choruses assemble.*

**CHORUS OF MEN**

> I have a simple
> tale to relate you,
> a sterling example
> of masculine virtue:

> The huntsman bold Melanion
>     was once a harried quarry.
> The women in town tracked him down
>     and badgered him to marry.

> Melanion knew the cornered male
>     eventually cohabits.
> Assessing the odds, he took to the woods
>     and lived by trapping rabbits.

> He stuck to the virgin stand, sustained
>     by rabbit meat and hate,
> and never returned, but ever remained
>     an alfresco celibate.

> Melanion is our ideal;
>     his loathing makes us free.
> Our dearest aim is the gemlike flame
>     of his misogyny.

**OLD MAN**

> Let me kiss that wizened cheek. . . .

**OLD WOMAN**

*Threatening with a fist.*

> A wish too rash for that withered flesh.

**OLD MAN**

> and lay you low with a highflying kick.

*He tries one and misses.*

**OLD WOMAN**

> Exposing an overgrown underbrush.

OLD MAN

A hairy behind, historically, means
    masculine force: Myronides
harassed the foe with his mighty mane,
    and furry Phormion swept the seas
        of enemy ships, never meeting his match—
            such was the nature of his thatch.

CHORUS OF WOMEN

            I offer an anecdote
            for your opinion,
            an adequate antidote
            for your Melanion:

        Timon, the noted local grouch,
            put rusticating hermits
    out of style by building his wilds
            inside the city limits.

        He shooed away society
            with natural battlements:
    his tongue was edgèd; his shoulder, frigid;
            his beard, a picket fence.

        When random contacts overtaxed him,
            he didn't stop to pack,
    but loaded curses on the male of the species,
            left town, and never came back.

        Timon, you see, was a misanthrope
            in a properly narrow sense:
    his spleen was vented only on men . . .
            *we* were his dearest friends.

OLD WOMAN

*Making a fist.*

        Enjoy a chop to that juiceless chin?

OLD MAN

*Backing away.*

        I'm jolted already. Thank you, no.

**OLD WOMAN**

Perhaps a trip from a well-turned shin?

*She tries a kick and misses.*

**OLD MAN**

Brazenly baring the mantrap below.

**OLD WOMAN**

At least it's *neat.* I'm not too sorry
to have you see my daintiness.
My habits are still depilatory;
age hasn't made me a bristly mess.
Secure in my smoothness, I'm never in doubt—
though even down is out.

*Lysistrata mounts the platform and scans the horizon. When her gaze reaches the left, she stops suddenly.*

**LYSISTRATA**

Ladies, attention! Battle stations, please!
And quickly!

*A general rush of women to the battlements.*

**KLEONIKE**

What is it?

**MYRRHINE**

What's all the shouting for?

**LYSISTRATA**

A MAN!

*Consternation.*

Yes, it's a man. And he's coming this way!
Hmm. Seems to have suffered a seizure. Broken out
with a nasty attack of love.

*Prayer, aside.*

O Aphrodite,
Mistress all-victorious,

> mysterious, voluptuous,
> you who make the crooked straight . . .
> don't let this happen to US!

**KLEONIKE**

I don't care who he is—*where is he?*

**LYSISTRATA**

*Pointing.*

                                   Down there—
just flanking that temple—Demeter the Fruitful.

**KLEONIKE**

                                            My.

Definitely a man.

**MYRRHINE**

*Craning for a look.*

                 I wonder who it can be?

**LYSISTRATA**

See for yourselves.—Can anyone identify him?

**MYRRHINE**

Oh lord, I can.
                 *That* is my husband—Kinesias.*

**LYSISTRATA**

*To Myrrhine.*

Your duty is clear.
                 Pop him on the griddle, twist
the spit, braize him, baste him, stew him in his own
juice, do him to a turn. Sear him with kisses,
coyness, caresses, *everything*—
                                   but stop where Our Oath
begins.

**MYRRHINE**

    Relax. I can take care of this.

**LYSISTRATA**

Of course
you can, dear. Still, a little help can't hurt, now
can it? I'll just stay around for a bit
and—er—poke up the fire.
—Everyone else inside!

*Exit all the women but Lysistrata, on the platform, and Myrrhine, who stands near the Akropolis entrance, hidden from her husband's view. Kinesias staggers on, in erection and considerable pain, followed by a male slave who carries a baby boy.*

**KINESIAS**

OUCH!!
Omigod.
Hypertension, twinges. . . . I can't hold out much more.
I'd rather be dismembered.
*How long, ye gods, how long?*

**LYSISTRATA**

*Officially.*

WHO GOES THERE?
WHO PENETRATES OUR POSITIONS?

**KINESIAS**

Me.

**LYSISTRATA**

A Man?

**KINESIAS**

Every inch.

**LYSISTRATA**

Then inch yourself out
of here. Off Limits to Men.

**KINESIAS**

This *is* the limit.
Just who are *you* to throw me out?

**LYSISTRATA**

The Lookout.

**KINESIAS**

Well, look here, Lookout. I'd like to see Myrrhine.
How's the outlook?

**LYSISTRATA**

Unlikely. Bring Myrrhine
to you? The idea!
Just by the by, who are you?

**KINESIAS**

A private citizen. Her husband, Kinesias.

**LYSISTRATA**

No!
Meeting you—I'm overcome!
Your name, you know,
is not without its fame among us girls.

*Aside.*

—Matter of fact, we have a name for *it*.—
I swear, you're never out of Myrrhine's mouth.
She won't even nibble a quince, or swallow an egg,
without reciting, "Here's to Kinesias!"

**KINESIAS**

For god's sake,
will you . . .

**LYSISTRATA**

*Sweeping on over his agony.*

Word of honor, it's true. Why, when
we discuss our husbands (you know how women are),
Myrrhine refuses to argue. She simply insists:
"Compared with Kinesias, the rest have *nothing!*"
Imagine!

**KINESIAS**

*Bring her out here!*

**LYSISTRATA**

Really? And what would I
get out of this?

**KINESIAS**

You see my situation. I'll raise
whatever I can. This can all be yours.

**LYSISTRATA**

Goodness.
It's really her place. I'll go and get her.

*She descends from the platform and moves to Myrrhine,
out of Kinesias' sight.*

**KINESIAS**

Speed!
—Life is a husk. She left our home, and happiness
went with her. Now pain is the tenant. Oh, to enter
that wifeless house, to sense that awful emptiness,
to eat that tasteless, joyle s food—it makes
it hard, I tell you.
Harder all the time.

**MYRRHINE**

*Still out of his sight, in a voice to be overheard.*

Oh, I *do* love him! I'm mad about him! But he
doesn't want my love. Please don't make me see him.

**KINESIAS**

Myrrhine darling, why do you *act* this way?
Come down here!

**MYRRHINE**

*Appearing at the wall.*

Down there? Certainly not!

**KINESIAS**

It's me, Myrrhine. I'm begging you. Please come down.

**MYRRHINE**

I don't see why you're begging me. You don't need me.

**KINESIAS**

I don't need you? I'm at the end of my rope!

**MYRRHINE**

I'm leaving.

*She turns. Kinesias grabs the boy from the slave.*

**KINESIAS**

No! Wait! At least you'll have to listen
to the voice of your child.

*To the boy, in a fierce undertone.*

—(Call your mother!)

*Silence.*

. . . to the voice
of your very own child . . .

—(Call your mother, brat!)

**CHILD**

MOMMYMOMMYMOMMY!

**KINESIAS**

Where's your maternal instinct? He hasn't been washed
or fed for a week. How can you be so pitiless?

**MYRRHINE**

*Him* I pity. Of all the pitiful excuses
for a father. . . .

**KINESIAS**

Come down here, dear. For the baby's sake.

**MYRRHINE**

Motherhood! I'll have to come. I've got no choice.

**KINESIAS**

*Soliloquizing as she descends.*

It may be me, but I'll swear she looks years younger—
and gentler—her eyes caress me. And then they flash:
that anger, that verve, that high-and-mighty air!
She's fire, she's ice—and I'm stuck right in the middle.

**MYRRHINE**

*Taking the baby.*

Sweet babykins with such a nasty daddy!
Here, let Mummy kissums. Mummy's little darling.

**KINESIAS**

*The injured husband.*

You should be ashamed of yourself, letting those women
lead you around. Why do you DO these things?
You only make me suffer and hurt your poor,
sweet self.

**MYRRHINE**

Keep your hands away from me!

**KINESIAS**

But the house, the furniture, everything we own—you're
letting it go to hell!

**MYRRHINE**

Frankly, I couldn't care less.

**KINESIAS**

But your weaving's unraveled—the loom is full of
chickens! You couldn't care less about *that?*

**MYRRHINE**

>                     I certainly couldn't.

**KINESIAS**

And the holy rites of Aphrodite? Think how long
that's been.
>                     Come on, darling, let's go home.

**MYRRHINE**

I absolutely refuse!
>                     Unless you agree to a truce
to stop the war.

**KINESIAS**

>                     Well, then, if that's your decision,
we'll STOP the war!

**MYRRHINE**

>                     Well, then, if that's your decision,
I'll come back—*after* it's done.
>                     But, for the present,
I've sworn off.

**KINESIAS**

>                     At least lie down for a minute.
We'll talk.

**MYRRHINE**

>               I know what you're up to—NO!
—And yet. . . . I really can't say I don't love you . . .

**KINESIAS**

>                                     You love me?
So what's the trouble? *Lie down.*

**MYRRHINE**

>                         Don't be disgusting.
In front of the baby?

**KINESIAS**

Er . . . no. Heaven Forfend.

*Taking the baby and pushing it at the slave.*

—Take this home.

*The slave obeys.*

—Well, darling, we're rid of the kid . . .
let's go to bed!

**MYRRHINE**

Poor dear.

But where does one do
this sort of thing?

**KINESIAS**

Where? All we need is a little
nook. . . . We'll try Pan's grotto. Excellent spot.

**MYRRHINE**

*With a nod at the Akropolis.*

I'll have to be pure to get back in *there*. How can I
expunge my pollution?

**KINESIAS**

Sponge off in the pool next door.

**MYRRHINE**

I did swear an Oath. I'm supposed to perjure myself?

**KINESIAS**

Bother the Oath. Forget it—I'll take the blame.

*A pause.*

**MYRRHINE**

Now I'll go get us a cot.

**KINESIAS**

No! Not a cot!
The ground's enough for us.

**MYRRHINE**

> *I'll get the cot.*
For all your faults, I refuse to put you to bed
in the dirt.

*She exits into the Akropolis.*

**KINESIAS**

> She certainly loves me. That's nice to know.

**MYRRHINE**

*Returning with a rope-tied cot.*

Here. You hurry to bed while I undress.

*Kinesias lies down.*

Gracious me—I forgot. We need a mattress.

**KINESIAS**

Who wants a mattress? Not me!

**MYRRHINE**

> Oh, yes, you do.
It's perfectly squalid on the ropes.

**KINESIAS**

> Well, give me a kiss
to tide me over.

**MYRRHINE**

> *Voilà.*

*She pecks at him and leaves.*

**KINESIAS**

> OoolaLAlala!
—Make it a quick trip, dear.

**MYRRHINE**

*Entering with the mattress, she waves Kinesias off the cot
and lays the mattress on it.*

Here we are.
Our mattress. Now hurry to bed while I undress.

*Kinesias lies down again.*

Gracious me—I forgot. You don't have a pillow.

**KINESIAS**

I do *not* need a pillow.

**MYRRHINE**

I know, but *I* do.

*She leaves.*

**KINESIAS**

What a lovefeast! Only the table gets laid.*

**MYRRHINE**

*Returning with a pillow.*

Rise and shine!

*Kinesias jumps up. She places the pillow.*

And now I have everything I need.

**KINESIAS**

*Lying down again.*

You certainly do.
Come here, my little jewelbox!

**MYRRHINE**

Just taking off my bra.
Don't break your promise:
no cheating about the Peace.

**KINESIAS**

I swear to god,
I'll die first!

**MYRRHINE**

*Coming to him.*

Just look. You don't have a blanket.

**KINESIAS**

I didn't plan to go camping—I want to make love!

**MYRRHINE**

Relax. You'll get your love. I'll be right back.

*She leaves.*

**KINESIAS**

Relax? I'm dying a slow death by dry goods!

**MYRRHINE**

*Returning with the blanket.*

Get up!

**KINESIAS**

*Getting out of bed.*

I've been up for hours. I was up before I was up.

*Myrrhine spreads the blanket on the mattress, and he lies down again.*

**MYRRHINE**

I presume you want perfume?

**KINESIAS**

Positively NO!

**MYRRHINE**

Absolutely *yes*—whether you want it or not.

*She leaves.*

**KINESIAS**

Dear Zeus, I don't ask for much—but please let her spill it.

**MYRRHINE**

*Returning with a bottle.*

Hold out your hand like a good boy.

Now rub it in.

**KINESIAS**

*Obeying and sniffing.*

> *This* is to quicken desire? Too strong. It grabs
> your nose and bawls out: *Try again tomorrow.*

**MYRRHINE**

> I'm *awful!* I brought you that rancid Rhodian brand.

*She starts off with the bottle.*

**KINESIAS**

> This is just *lovely.* Leave it, woman!

**MYRRHINE**

> Silly!

*She leaves.*

**KINESIAS**

> God damn the clod who first concocted perfume!

**MYRRHINE**

*Returning with another bottle.*

> Here, try this flask.

**KINESIAS**

> Thanks—but you try mine.
> Come to bed, you witch—
> and please stop bringing
> things!

**MYRRHINE**

> *That* is exactly what I'll do.
> There go my shoes.
> Incidentally, darling, you *will*
> remember to vote for the truce?

**KINESIAS**

**I'LL THINK IT OVER!**

*Myrrhine runs off for good.*

That woman's laid me waste—destroyed me, root
and branch!
>    I'm scuttled,
>        gutted,
>            up the spout!
And Myrrhine's gone!

*In a parody of a tragic kommos.*

>    Out upon't! But how? But where?
>    Now I have lost the fairest fair,
>    how screw my courage to yet another
>    sticking-place? Aye, there's the rub—
>    And yet, this wagging, wanton babe
>    must soon be laid to rest, or else . . .
>    Ho, Pandar!
>        Pandar!
>            I'd hire a nurse.

**KORYPHAIOS OF MEN**

>    Grievous your bereavement, cruel
>    the slow tabescence of your soul.
>    I bid my liquid pity mingle.

>    Oh, where the soul, and where, alack!
>    the cod to stand the taut attack
>    of swollen prides, the scorching tensions
>    that ravine up the lumbar regions?
>        His morning lay
>        has gone astray.

**KINESIAS**

*In agony.*

>    O Zeus, reduce the throbs, the throes!

**KORYPHAIOS OF MEN**

>    I turn my tongue to curse the cause
>    of your affliction—that jade, that slut,
>    that hag, that ogress . . .

KINESIAS

>>>>>>> No! Slight not
>> my light-o'-love, my dove, my sweet!

KORYPHAIOS OF MEN

>>>>> Sweet!
>>>>>>> O Zeus who rul'st the sky,
>> snatch that slattern up on high,
>> crack thy winds, unleash thy thunder,
>> tumble her over, trundle her under,
>> juggle her from hand to hand;
>> twirl her ever near the ground—
>> drop her in a well-aimed fall
>> on our comrade's tool! That's all.

*Kinesias exits left.*

*A Spartan Herald enters from the right, holding his cloak together in a futile attempt to conceal his condition.*

HERALD

This Athens? Where-all kin I find the Council of Elders or else the Executive Board? I brung some news.

*The Commissioner,\* swathed in his cloak, enters from the left.*

COMMISSIONER

And what are you—a man? a signpost? a joint-stock company?

HERALD

>> A herald, sonny, a honest-to-Kastor
herald. I come to chat 'bout thet-there truce.

COMMISSIONER

. . . carrying a concealed weapon? Pretty underhanded.

HERALD

*Twisting to avoid the Commissioner's direct gaze.*

Hain't done no sech a thang!

**COMMISSIONER**

> Very well, stand still.
Your cloak's out of crease—hernia? Are the roads that
  bad?

**HERALD**

I swear this feller's plumb tetched in the haid!

**COMMISSIONER**

*Throwing open the Spartan's cloak, exposing the phallus.*

> You clown,
you've got an erection!

**HERALD**

*Wildly embarrassed.*

> Hain't got no sech a thang!
You stop this-hyer foolishment!

**COMMISSIONER**

> What *have* you got there, then?

**HERALD**

Thet-thur's a Spartan *e*pistle.* In code.

**COMMISSIONER**

> I have the key.

*Throwing open his cloak.*

Behold another Spartan *e*pistle. In code.

*Tiring of teasing.*

> Let's get down to cases. I know the score,
so tell me the truth.
> How are things with you in Sparta?

**HERALD**

Thangs is up in the air. The whole Alliance
is purt-near 'bout to explode. We-uns'll need barrels,
'stead of women.

**COMMISSIONER**

What was the cause of this outburst?
The great god Pan?

**HERALD**

Nope. I'll lay 'twere Lampito,
most likely. She begun, and then they was off
and runnin' at the post in a bunch, every last little gal
in Sparta, drivin' their menfolk away from the winner's
circle.

**COMMISSIONER**

How are you taking this?

**HERALD**

Painful-like.
Everyone's doubled up worse as a midget nursin'
a wick in a midnight wind come moon-dark time.
Cain't even tetch them little old gals on the moosey
without we all agree to a Greece-wide Peace.

**COMMISSIONER**

Of course!
A universal female plot—all Hellas
risen in rebellion—I should have known!
Return
to Sparta with this request:
Have them despatch us
a Plenipotentiary Commission, fully empowered
to conclude an armistice. I have full confidence
that I can persuade our Senate to do the same,
without extending myself. The evidence is at hand.

**HERALD**

I'm a-flyin', Sir! I hev never heered your equal!

*Exeunt hurriedly, the Commissioner to the left, the Herald
to the right.*

KORYPHAIOS OF MEN

> The most unnerving work of nature,*
> the pride of applied immorality,
> is the common female human.
> No fire can match, no beast can best her.
> O Unsurmountability,
> thy name—worse luck—is Woman.

KORYPHAIOS OF WOMEN

> After such knowledge, why persist
> in wearing out this feckless
> war between the sexes?
> When can I apply for the post
> of ally, partner, and general friend?

KORYPHAIOS OF MEN

> I won't be ployed to revise, re-do,
> amend, extend, or bring to an end
> my irreversible credo:
> *Misogyny Forever!*
> —The answer's never.

KORYPHAIOS OF WOMEN

> All right. Whenever you choose.
> But, for the present, I refuse
> to let you look your absolute worst,
> parading around like an unfrocked freak:
> I'm coming over and get you dressed.

*She dresses him in his tunic, an action (like others in this scene) imitated by the members of the Chorus of Women toward their opposite numbers in the Chorus of Men.*

KORYPHAIOS OF MEN

> This seems sincere. It's not a trick.
> Recalling the rancor with which I stripped,
> I'm overlaid with chagrin.

KORYPHAIOS OF WOMEN

> Now you resemble a man,
> not some ghastly practical joke.

And if you show me a little respect
(and promise not to kick), I'll extract
the beast in you.

**KORYPHAIOS OF MEN**

*Searching himself.*

What beast in me?

**KORYPHAIOS OF WOMEN**

That insect. There. The bug that's stuck
in your eye.

**KORYPHAIOS OF MEN**

*Playing along dubiously.*

This gnat?

**KORYPHAIOS OF WOMEN**

Yes, nitwit!

**KORYPHAIOS OF MEN**

Of course.

That steady, festering agony. . . .
You've put your finger on the source
of all my lousy troubles. Please
roll back the lid and scoop it out.
I'd like to see it.

**KORYPHAIOS OF WOMEN**

All right, I'll do it.

*Removing the imaginary insect.*

Although, of all the impossible cranks. . . .
Do you sleep in a swamp? Just look at this.
I've never seen a bigger chigger.

**KORYPHAIOS OF MEN**

Thanks.
Your kindness touches me deeply. For years,

that thing's been sinking wells in my eye.
Now you've unplugged me. Here come the tears.

KORYPHAIOS OF WOMEN

I'll dry your tears, though I can't say why.

*Wiping away the tears.*

Of all the irresponsible boys. . . .
*And* I'll kiss you.

KORYPHAIOS OF MEN

Don't you kiss me!

KORYPHAIOS OF WOMEN

What made you think you had a choice?

*She kisses him.*

KORYPHAIOS OF MEN

All right, damn you, that's enough of that ingrained
    palaver.
I can't dispute the truth or logic of the pithy old proverb:
        *Life with women is hell.*
        *Life without women is hell, too.*
And so we conclude a truce with you, on the following
    terms:
in future, a mutual moratorium on mischief in all its
    forms.
Agreed?—Let's make a single chorus and start our song.

*The two Choruses unite and face the audience.*

CHORUS OF MEN*

We're not about to introduce
the standard personal abuse—
        the Choral Smear
Of Present Persons (usually,
in every well-made comedy,
        inserted here).
Instead, in deed and utterance, we

shall now indulge in philanthropy
    because we feel
that members of the audience
endure, in the course of current events,
    sufficient hell.
Therefore, friends, be rich! Be flush!
Apply to us, and borrow cash
    in large amounts.
The Treasury stands behind us—there—
and we can personally take care
    of small accounts.
Drop up today. Your credit's good.
Your loan won't have to be repaid
    in full until
the war is over. And then, your debt
is only the money you actually get—
    nothing at all.

CHORUS OF WOMEN

Just when we meant to entertain
some madcap gourmets from out of town
    —such flawless taste!—
the present unpleasantness intervened,
and now we fear the feast we planned
    will go to waste.
The soup is waiting, rich and thick;
I've sacrificed a suckling pig
    —the pièce de résistance—
whose toothsome cracklings should amaze
the most fastidious gourmets—
    you, for instance.
To everybody here, I say
take potluck at my house today
    with me and mine.
Bathe and change as fast as you can,
bring the children, hurry down,
    and walk right in.
Don't bother to knock. No need at all.
My house is yours. Liberty Hall.
    What are friends for?
Act self-possessed when you come over;

it may help out when you discover
I've locked the door.

*A delegation of Spartans enters from the right, with difficulty. They have removed their cloaks, but hold them before themselves in an effort to conceal their condition.*

KORYPHAIOS OF MEN

What's this? Behold the Spartan ambassadors,
  dragging their beards,
pussy-footing along. It appears they've developed
  a hitch in the crotch.

*Advancing to greet them.*

Men of Sparta, I bid you welcome!
                                And now
to the point: What predicament brings you among us?

SPARTAN

We-uns is up a stump. Hain't fit fer chatter.

*Flipping aside his cloak.*

Here's our predicament. Take a look for yourselfs.

KORYPHAIOS OF MEN

Well, I'll be damned—a regular disaster area.
Inflamed. I imagine the temperature's rather intense?

SPARTAN

Hit ain't the heat, hit's the tumidity.
                                But words
won't help what ails us. We-uns come after Peace.
Peace from any person, at any price.

*Enter the Athenian delegation from the left, led by Kinesias.\* They are wearing cloaks, but are obviously in as much travail as the Spartans.*

KORYPHAIOS OF MEN

Behold our local Sons of the Soil, stretching
their garments away from their groins, like wrestlers.
Grappling with their plight. Some sort of athlete's disease,

no doubt.
An outbreak of epic proportions.

                              Athlete's foot?

No. Could it be athlete's . . . ?

KINESIAS

*Breaking in.*

                              Who can tell us
how to get hold of Lysistrata? We've come as delegates
to the Sexual Congress.

*Opening his cloak.*

                    Here are our credentials.

KORYPHAIOS OF MEN

*Ever the scientist, looking from the Athenians to the Spartans and back again.*

The words are different, but the malady seems the same.

*To Kinesias.*

Dreadful disease. When the crisis reaches its height,
what do you take for it?

KINESIAS

                    Whatever comes to hand.
But now we've reached the bitter end. It's Peace
or we fall back on Kleisthenes.

                              And he's got a waiting list.

KORYPHAIOS OF MEN

*To the Spartans.*

Take my advice and put your clothes on. If someone
from that self-appointed Purity League* comes by, you
may be docked. They do it to the statues of Hermes,
they'll do it to you.

**KINESIAS**

*Since he has not yet noticed the Spartans, he interprets the warning as meant for him, and hurriedly pulls his cloak together, as do the other Athenians.*

        Excellent advice.

**SPARTAN**

                  Hit shorely is.
Hain't nothing to argue after. Let's git dressed.

*As they put on their cloaks, the Spartans are finally noticed by Kinesias.*

**KINESIAS**

Welcome, men of Sparta! This is a shameful
disgrace to masculine honor.

**SPARTAN**

                    Hit could be worser.
Ef them Herm-choppers seed us all fired up,
they'd *really* take us down a peg or two.

**KINESIAS**

Gentlemen, let's descend to details. Specifically,
why are you here?

**SPARTAN**

                  Ambassadors. We come to dicker
'bout thet-thur Peace.

**KINESIAS**

                  Perfect! Precisely our purpose.
Let's send for Lysistrata. Only she can reconcile
our differences. There'll be no Peace for us without her.

**SPARTAN**

We-uns ain't fussy. Call Lysistratos, too, if you want.

*The gates to the Akropolis open, and Lysistrata emerges, accompanied by her handmaid, Peace—a beautiful girl without a stitch on. Peace remains out of sight by the gates until summoned.*

**KORYPHAIOS OF MEN**

Hail, most virile of women! Summon up all your
 experience:
Be terrible and tender,
     lofty and lowbrow,
        severe and demure.
Here stand the Leaders of Greece, enthralled by your
 charm.
They yield the floor to you and submit their claims for
 your arbitration.

**LYSISTRATA**

Really, it shouldn't be difficult, if I can catch them
all bothered, before they start to solicit each other.
I'll find out soon enough. Where's Peace?
        —Come here.

*Peace moves from her place by the gates to Lysistrata. The
delegations goggle at her.*

Now, dear, first get those Spartans and bring them to me.
Take them by the hand, but don't be pushy about it,
not like our husbands (no savoir-faire at all!).
Be a lady, be proper, do just what you'd do at home:
if hands are refused, conduct them by the handle.

*Peace leads the Spartans to a position near Lysistrata.*

And now a hand to the Athenians—it doesn't matter
where; accept any offer—and bring *them* over.

*Peace conducts the Athenians to a position near Lysistrata,
opposite the Spartans.*

You Spartans move up closer—right *here*—

*To the Athenians.*

             and *you*
stand over *here*.
    —And now attend my speech.

*This the delegations do with some difficulty, because of the
conflicting attractions of Peace, who is standing beside her
mistress.*

> I am a woman—but not without some wisdom:
> my native wit is not completely negligible,
> and I've listened long and hard to the discourse of my
> elders—my education is not entirely despicable.
>
> > > > > > > Well,
> now that I've got you, I intend to give you hell,
> and I'm perfectly right. Consider your actions:
>
> > > > > > > > At festivals,
> in Pan-Hellenic harmony, like true blood-brothers, you
> > share
> the selfsame basin of holy water, and sprinkle
> altars all over Greece—Olympia, Delphoi,
> Thermopylai . . . (I could go on and on, if length
> were my only object.)
>
> > > > > But now, when the Persians sit by
> and wait, in the very presence of your enemies, you fight
> each other, destroy *Greek* men, destroy *Greek* cities!
> —Point One of my address is now concluded.

**KINESIAS**

*Gazing at Peace.*

> I'm destroyed, if this is drawn out much longer!

**LYSISTRATA**

*Serenely unconscious of the interruption.*

> —Men of Sparta, I direct these remarks to you.
> Have you forgotten that a Spartan suppliant once came
> to beg assistance from Athens? Recall Perikleidas:
> Fifty years ago, he clung to our altar,
> his face dead-white above his crimson robe, and pleaded
> for an army. Messene was pressing you hard in revolt,
> and to this upheaval, Poseidon, the Earthshaker, added
> another.
>
> > > > But Kimon took four thousand troops

from Athens—an army which saved the state of Sparta.
Such treatment have you received at the hands of Athens,
you who devastate the country that came to your aid!

**KINESIAS**

*Stoutly; the condemnation of his enemy has made him for-
get the girl momentarily.*

You're right, Lysistrata. The Spartans are clearly in the
wrong!

**SPARTAN**

*Guiltily backing away from Peace, whom he has attempted
to pat.*

Hit's wrong, I reckon, but that's the purtiest behind . . .

**LYSISTRATA**

*Turning to the Athenians.*

—Men of Athens, do you think I'll let *you* off?
Have you forgotten the Tyrant's days,* when you wore
the smock of slavery, when the Spartans turned to the
spear, cut down the pride of Thessaly, despatched the
friends of tyranny, and dispossessed your oppressors?
                           Recall:
On that great day, your only allies were Spartans;
your liberty came at their hands, which stripped away
your servile garb and clothed you again in Freedom!

**SPARTAN**

*Indicating Lysistrata.*

Hain't never seed no higher type of woman.

**KINESIAS**

*Indicating Peace.*

Never saw one I wanted so much to top.

LYSISTRATA

*Oblivious to the byplay, addressing both groups.*

With such a history of mutual benefits conferred
and received, why are you fighting? Stop this wickedness!
Come to terms with each other! What prevents you?

SPARTAN

We'd a heap sight druther make Peace, if we was
indemnified with a plumb strategic location.

*Pointing at Peace's rear.*

We'll take thet butte.

LYSISTRATA

Butte?

SPARTAN

The Promontory of Pylos—Sparta's Back Door.
We've missed it fer a turrible spell.

*Reaching.*

Hev to keep our
hand in.

KINESIAS

*Pushing him away.*

The price is too high—you'll never take that!

LYSISTRATA

Oh, let them have it.

KINESIAS

What room will we have left
for maneuvers?

LYSISTRATA

Demand another spot in exchange.

**KINESIAS**

*Surveying Peace like a map as he addresses the Spartan.*

Then you hand over to us—uh, let me see—
let's try Thessaly*—

*Indicating the relevant portions of Peace.*

First of all, Easy Mountain . . .
then the Maniac Gulf behind it . . .

and down to Megara
for the legs . . .

**SPARTAN**

You cain't take all of thet! Yore plumb
out of yore mind!

**LYSISTRATA**

*To Kinesias.*

Don't argue. Let the legs go.

*Kinesias nods. A pause. General smiles of agreement.*

**KINESIAS**

*Doffing his cloak.*

I feel an urgent desire to plow a few furrows.

**SPARTAN**

*Doffing his cloak.*

Hit's time to work a few loads of fertilizer in.

**LYSISTRATA**

Conclude the treaty and the simple life is yours.
If such is your decision convene your councils,
and then deliberate the matter with your allies.

**KINESIAS**

*Deliberate? Allies?*

We're over-extended already!
Wouldn't every ally approve our position—
*Union Now?*

SPARTAN

>I know I kin speak for ourn.

KINESIAS

And I for ours.
>They're just a bunch of gigolos.

LYSISTRATA

I heartily approve.
>Now first attend to your purification,
then we, the women, will welcome you to the Citadel
and treat you to all the delights of a home-cooked
banquet. Then you'll exchange your oaths and pledge
your faith, and every man of you will take his wife and
depart for home.

*Lysistrata and Peace enter the Akropolis.*

KINESIAS

>Let's hurry!

SPARTAN

>Lead on, everwhich
way's yore pleasure.

KINESIAS

>This way, then—and HURRY!

*The delegations exeunt at a run.*

CHORUS OF WOMEN

>I'd never stint on anybody.
>And now I include, in my boundless bounty,
>>the younger set.
>Attention, you parents of teenage girls
>about to debut in the social whirl.
>>Here's what you get:
>Embroidered linens, lush brocades,

a huge assortment of ready-mades,
> from mantles to shifts;
*plus* bracelets and bangles of solid gold—
every item my wardrobe holds—
> absolute gifts!
Don't miss this offer. Come to my place,
barge right in, and make your choice.
> You can't refuse.
Everything there must go today.
Finders keepers—cart it away!
> How can you lose?
Don't spare me. Open all the locks.
Break every seal. Empty every box.
> Keep ferreting—
And your sight's considerably better than mine
if you should possibly chance to find
> a single thing.

CHORUS OF MEN

Troubles, friend? Too many mouths
to feed, and not a scrap in the house
> to see you through?
Faced with starvation? Don't give it a thought.
Pay attention; I'll tell you what
> I'm gonna do.
I overbought. I'm overstocked.
Every room in my house is clogged
> with flour (best ever),
glutted with luscious loaves whose size
you wouldn't believe. I need the space;
> do me a favor:
Bring gripsacks, knapsacks, duffle bags,
pitchers, cisterns, buckets, and kegs
> around to me.
A courteous servant will see to your needs;
he'll fill them up with A-1 wheat—
> and all for free!
—Oh. Just one final word before
you turn your steps to my front door:
> I happen to own

a dog. Tremendous animal.
Can't stand a leash. And bites likc hell—
    better stay home.

*The united Chorus flocks to the door of the Akropolis.**

KORYPHAIOS OF MEN

*Banging at the door.*

    Hey, open up in there!

*The door opens, and the Commissioner appears. He wears
a wreath, carries a torch, and is slightly drunk. He addresses
the Koryphaios.*

COMMISSIONER

                        You know the Regulations.
Move along!

*He sees the entire Chorus.*

            —And why are YOU lounging around?
I'll wield my trusty torch and scorch the lot!

*The Chorus backs away in mock horror. He stops and looks
at his torch.*

    —*This* is the bottom of the barrel. A cheap burlesque bit.
I refuse to do it. I have my pride.

*With a start, he looks at the audience, as though hearing
a protest. He shrugs and addresses the audience.*

                        —No choice, eh?
Well, if that's the way it is, we'll take the trouble.
Anything to keep you happy.

*The Chorus advances eagerly.*

KORYPHAIOS OF MEN

                        Don't forget us!
We're in this, too. Your trouble is ours!

COMMISSIONER

*Resuming his character and jabbing with his torch at the Chorus.*

> Keep moving!
Last man out of the way goes home without hair!
Don't block the exit. Give the Spartans some room.
They've dined in comfort; let them go home in peace.

*The Chorus shrinks back from the door. Kinesias, wreathed and quite drunk, appears at the door. He speaks his first speech in Spartan.**

KINESIAS

Hain't never seed sech a spread! Hit were splendiferous!

COMMISSIONER

I gather the Spartans won friends and influenced people?

KINESIAS

And *we've* never been so brilliant. It was the wine.

COMMISSIONER

Precisely.

> The reason? A sober Athenian is just
*non compos.* If I can carry a little proposal
I have in mind, our Foreign Service will flourish,
guided by this rational rule:

> *No Ambassador
Without a Skinful.*

> Reflect on our past performance:
Down to a Spartan parley we troop, in a state
of disgusting sobriety, looking for trouble. It muddles
our senses: we read between the lines; we hear,
not what the Spartans say, but what we suspect
they might have been about to be going to say.
We bring back paranoid reports—cheap fiction, the fruit
of temperance. Cold-water diplomacy, pah!

> Contrast
this evening's total pleasure, the free-and-easy

give-and-take of friendship: If we were singing,
> *Just Kleitagora and me,*
> *Alone in Thessaly,*

and someone missed his cue and cut in loudly,
> *Ajax, son of Telamon,*
> *He was one hell of a man—*

no one took it amiss, or started a war;
we clapped him on the back and gave three cheers.

*During this recital, the Chorus has sidled up to the door.*

—Dammit, are you back here again?

*Waving his torch.*

> Scatter!

Get out of the road! Gangway, you gallowsbait!

**KINESIAS**

Yes, everyone out of the way. They're coming out.

*Through the door emerge the Spartan delegation, a flutist, the Athenian delegation, Lysistrata, Kleonike, Myrrhine, and the rest of the women from the citadel, both Athenian and Peloponnesian. The Chorus splits into its male and female components and draws to the sides to give the procession room.*

**SPARTAN**

*To the flutist.*

Friend and kinsman, take up them pipes a yourn.
I'd like fer to shuffle a bit and sing a right sweet
song in honor of Athens and us'uns, too.

**COMMISSIONER**

*To the flutist.*

Marvelous, marvelous—come, take up your pipes!

*To the Spartan.*

I certainly love to see you Spartans dance.

*The flutist plays, and the Spartan begins a slow dance.*

**SPARTAN**

Memory,
send me
your Muse,
who knows
our glory,
knows Athens'—
Tell the story:
At Artemision
like gods, they stampeded
the hulks of the Medes, and
beat them.

And Leonidas
leading us—
the wild boars
whetting their tusks.
And the foam flowered,
flowered and flowed,
down our cheeks
to our knees below.
The Persians there
like the sands of the sea—

Hither, huntress,
virgin, goddess,
tracker, slayer,
to our truce!
Hold us ever
fast together;
bring our pledges
love and increase;
wean us from the
fox's wiles—

Hither, huntress!
Virgin, hither!

**LYSISTRATA***

*Surveying the assemblage with a proprietary air.*

Well, the preliminaries are over—very nicely, too.
So, Spartans,

*Indicating the Peloponnesian women who have been hostages.*

> take these girls back home. And *you*

*To the Athenian delegation, indicating the women from the Akropolis.*

> take *these* girls. Each man stand by his wife, each wife
> by her husband. Dance to the gods' glory, and thank
> them for the happy ending. And, from now on, please be
> careful. Let's not make the same mistakes again.

*The delegations obey; the men and women of the chorus join again for a rapid ode.*

CHORUS

> Start the chorus dancing,
> Summon all the Graces,
> Send a shout to Artemis in invocation.
> Call upon her brother,
> healer, chorus master,
> Call the blazing Bacchus, with his maddened muster.
>
> Call the flashing, fiery Zeus, and
> call his mighty, blessed spouse, and
> call the gods, call all the gods,
> to witness now and not forget
> our gentle, blissful Peace—the gift,
> the deed of Aphrodite.
> Ai!
> Alalai!   Paion!
> Leap you!   Paion!
> Victory!   Alalai!
> Hail!    Hail!    Hail!

LYSISTRATA
Spartan, let's have another song from you, a new one.

SPARTAN

> Leave darlin' Taygetos,
> Spartan Muse! Come to us

once more, flyin'
and glorifyin'
*Spartan* themes:
the god at Amyklai,
bronze-house Athene,
Tyndaros' twins,
the valiant ones,
playin' still by Eurotas' streams.

Up! Advance!
Leap to the dance!

Help us hymn Sparta,
lover of dancin',
lover of foot-pats,
where girls go prancin'
like fillies along Eurotas' banks,
whirlin' the dust, twinklin' their shanks,
shakin' their hair
like Maenads playin'
and jugglin' the thyrsis,
in frenzy obeyin'
Leda's daughter, the fair, the pure
Helen, the mistress of the choir.

Here, Muse, here!
Bind up your hair!

Stamp like a deer! Pound your feet!
Clap your hands! Give us a beat!

*Sing* the greatest,
*sing* the mightiest,
*sing* the conqueror,
*sing* to honor her—

Athene of the Bronze House!
Sing Athene!

*Exeunt omnes, dancing and singing.*

# Notes

page 16. *early morning:* The play's two time scales
should be noted. By one, its action encompasses
a day, beginning at dawn and lasting until after
sundown; by the other, its events logically oc-
cupy a period of weeks, if not months—not that
this sort of logic has much to do with the case.
At no point is the play stopped to indicate the
passage of time.

16. *Kleonike:* This is to adopt Wilamowitz' conjecture for the *Kalonike* of the manuscripts, without accepting his views on the character's age.
Kleonike's actions approach those of the stock
bibulous old woman too closely to indicate a
sweet young thing. She is older than Lysistrata,
who fits comfortably on the vague borderline
between "young matron" and "matron." Quite
a bit younger are Myrrhine and Lampito.

18. *those scrumptious eels:* The constant Athenian
gustatory passion, rendered sharper by the
War's embargo: eels from Lake Kopaïs in
Boiotia.

20. *hoisting her sandals:* This rendering follows,
with Coulon, Van Leeuwen's emendation at
64—τἀκάτειον "sail"—while suggesting that the
pun plays on the unmetrical reading of the
Ravennas, τἀκάτιον "skiff," as a name applied
to a woman's shoe. It is tempting to return to
an old proposal of Biset and read τἀκάτιον
ἀνήρετο.

20. *from the outskirts:* Literally, "from Anagyrous,"
a rural deme of Attika which took its name from
the plant *anagyros* "the stinking bean-trefoil."
Kleonike's riposte puns on this by reference to
an old proverb: "Well, the *anagyros* certainly
seems to have been disturbed"="you've really

stirred up a stink"="the fat's in the fire." Here, as often when geographical names are involved, it is more important to render the fact of a pun than the specifics of the original.

page 21. *I calklate so:* In employing a somewhat debased American mountain dialect to render the Laconic Greek of Lampito and her countrymen, I have tried to evoke something like the Athenian attitude toward their perennial enemies. They regarded the Spartans as formidably old-fashioned bumpkins, imperfectly civilized, possessed of a determined indifference to more modern value systems.

23. *Military waste:* Or perhaps treason. The Greek refers to a General Eukrates, who may be the brother of the illustrious and ill-starred Nikias. If so, he was put to death by the Thirty Tyrants in 404.

28. *in Athene's temple:* In the Opisthodomos, at the back of the Parthenon, was kept the reserve fund of one thousand silver talents established at the beginning of the War twenty years before. Since the fund had been dipped into during the previous year, Lampito's expression constitutes more than a normal exaggeration.

30. *The symbolism's too obscure:* This sentence may seem a startling expansion of the word *poi* (literally, "Whither?"; here, "What is the point of . . . ?"), but is in a good cause—an attempt to explain and motivate the darkest white horse in literature. The sequence is this: Lysistrata, annoyed at the interruption, sarcastically proposes a gaudy sacrifice; Kleonike, whose mind is proof against sarcasm, points out that it has nothing to do with the matter at hand. For the rationale, I am indebted to Wilamowitz, though he assigned the lines (191-93) differently. Other explanations, in terms of Amazons, genitalia, or lovemaking blueprints, are, albeit venerable,

obscure in themselves. One sympathizes with Rogers, who translated, "grey mare."

page 36. *Athene's statue:* Not one of Pheidias' colossal statues, but the old wooden figure of Athene Polias ("Guardian of the City") in the Erechtheion.

37. *right over there:* I have given the Koryphaios a bad memory and placed the object of his anger in the audience to point up what is happening. Rhodia, wife of the demagogue Lykon, was a real person, frequently lampooned for her morals. In a not unusual breaking of the dramatic illusion, her name occurs here as a surprise for the expected "Lysistrata." Some commentators, disliking surprises, have decided that Lysistrata is the wife of someone named Lykon—thus managing to ruin a joke and import an obscurity without the change of a word.

37. *expropriating our Akropolis:* Kleomenes' occupation of the Akropolis in 508, high point of his unsuccessful bid to help establish the Athenian aristocrats, lasted rather less than the six years which the Chorus seems to remember. The actual time was two days.

40. *at loggerheads over in Samos:* Most of the Athenian fleet was at the moment based in Samos, practically the only Ionian ally left to Athens, in order to make ready moves against those states who had defected to Sparta in 412 after the Sicilian fiasco.

42. *Hipponax swears by it:* The Greek refers to one Boupalos, a Chian sculptor mercilessly lampooned by the testy poet until, as a doubtful tradition has it, he hanged himself. The only surviving verse of Hipponax which bears on the subject ("Hold my clothes; I'll sock Boupalos in the jaw") does little to establish the tradition —or, indeed, to dispel the feeling that Hipponax was about as effective a boxer as the Koryphaios.

page 43. *for other bitches to gnaw:* I here adopt John
Jackson's transposition of line 363 to follow
367 (*Marginalia Scaenica*, p. 108).

43. *so lost to shame as Woman:* The observation
is clearly offered as an illustrative quotation,
and the sentiment is certainly Euripidean. But
the extant tragic line nearest it in expression is
Sophokles *Elektra* 622.

45. *A Commissioner of Public Safety:* That is, *a
proboulos,* one of the ten extraordinary Athenian officials appointed in 413 after the Sicilian
catastrophe as a check on legislative excesses.
Chiefly responsible for drafting the agenda of
Senate and Assembly, the commissioners were
drawn from men over forty years of age. The
two whose names we know were well along:
Hagnon was over sixty, Sophokles (if the poet
is meant, a matter not absolutely settled)
eighty-two. But these instances scarcely prove
Wilamowitz' contention that decrepitude was
a necessary qualification for the office; and
Aristophanes' Commissioner, for all his choleric
conservatism, is marked by vigor and intel-
lectual curiosity.

49. *goddess of the dew:* That is, Pandrosos, one of
the daughters of Athens' legendary King
Kekrops. A tutelary divinity in her own right,
she had a shrine in the Erechtheion—and was
never identified with Artemis. Having said this,
I follow in the translation an unprovable theory
of Rogers': that *pandrosos* "all-bedewing" just
might be an epithet of the moon-goddess, clas-
sical antiquity's best-attested virgin, who is
otherwise invoked here in three out of four
instances.

49. *ISMENIA:* As stated in the Introduction
(p. 13), I here assign two lines in Attic Greek
(447-48) to a Theban hostage, for no better
reason than symmetry.

53. *the Friends of Oligarchy:* This expansion makes

more explicit a reference to the political clubs, or *synōmosiai*, who caucussed and combined their votes to gain verdicts and offices, thus paving the road for the oligarchic upheaval in May of 411.

page 56. *Yᵉ menne must see to yᵉ warre:* Iliad 6.492 (Hektor to Andromache).

57. *"What Athens needs is a Man":* Traditionally interpreted (perhaps with too much enthusiasm) as a reference to the longing of the Athenian commonality for the return of glory-and-shame Alkibiades, who obliged the following summer.

59. *Pacifiers:* In the Greek, *Lysimachas* "Battle-settlers," a pun on the name of the heroine; also, if D. M. Lewis is right, a reference to her real-life model Lysimache—in 411, priestess of Athene.

61. *to snag important posts:* Most of this rather torturous allegory is self-explanatory, but the "clumps" are the political clubs, or "Friends of Oligarchy," mentioned earlier. See above, note to p. 53.

62. *To the audience:* Or, possibly, to the Chorus of Men. I do not accept Van Leeuwen's emendation here (598), but I do follow him in taking the line to be an interrupted exhortation to all available and qualified males.

62. *with her spindle:* Here and earlier, the women are certainly armed, but with what? The pronouns supplied by the Greek are tantalizingly specific in gender, but in nothing else; solutions usually bring out the worst in interpreters. I have tried to assign appropriate weapons early, and continue them to this denouement—but visualizers (or producers, if any there be) are at liberty, as elsewhere, to use their imaginations. One caveat: the Greek will not bear a direct repetition of the bath given earlier to the Old Men by the Old Women.

64. *my payroll:* The *triobolon*, the three-obol per

diem wage for jury duty, which often con-
stituted the only income of elderly men. It
would naturally be stored inside the Citadel
in the Treasury.

page 64. *WOMEN ticking off troops:* Emending πολίτας
at 626 to ὁπλίτας.

65. *Harmodios, Aristogeiton, and Me:* The reference, to a famous statuary group by the sculptor
Kritios in the Athenian Agora, picks up an
earlier quotation from a popular *skolion,* or
drinking-song, on the assassination of the tyrant
Hipparchos: "I'll carry my sword concealed in
a myrtle bough. . . ." The translation expands
on the idea, but hides the quotation in the
familiar "sword in olive branch."

65. *this proud progression:* Since this passage is
frequently cited as primary evidence for the
*cursus honorum* of a high-born young girl in
fifth-century Athens, here are the steps set forth
a bit more explicitly: (1) *arrêphoros* ("relic-
bearer") to Athene, one of four little girls who
carried the Goddess' sacred objects in Her
semi-annual festival of the *Arréphoria;* (2)
*aletris* ("mill-girl") to the Founding Mother
(doubtless Athene), one of the girls who ground
the meal to be made into sacrificial cakes; (3)
*arktos* ("she-bear") at the *Brauronia,* a festival
of Artemis held every fifth year at Brauron in
Attika, centering on a myth which told of the
killing of a tame bear sacred to that goddess;
and (4) *kanêphoros* ("basket-bearer"), the
maiden who bore the sacrificial cake and led
the procession at Athens' most important festivals, such as the City Dionysia and the Great
Panathenaia.

66. *the Mutual Funds from the Persian War:* This
money originally made up the treasury of the
Delian League, an alliance of Greek states
against Persia formed by the Athenian Aristeides
in 477; following its transfer, for safety's sake,

from the island of Delos to Athens in 454, it became for all practical purposes Athenian property, supported by tribute from the Allies. Athens' heavy expenses in Sicily, followed by the Allies' nonpayment and defection, made this question all too pointed in early 411.

*page* 67. *to the Heights:* To Leipsydrion, in the mountains north of Athens, where the besieged Alkmaionid exiles held out for a time against the forces of the tyrant Hippias. Since this siege, ever after symbolic of the Noble Lost Cause, took place in 513, commentators find it necessary to point out that the Chorus of Men couldn't *really* have fought in a battle 102 years before; that they are pretending, or speaking by extension for the Athenian Fighting Spirit, or whatever. Seemingly, this goes without saying; actually, it is dead wrong. Dramaturgy has little to do with geriatrics; Aristophanes needed a Chorus of Men old enough to be hidebound, decrepit, so old that they would first see the Women's Revolt, not in terms of sex, but of politics—the recrudescence of a personally experienced tyranny. He was cheerfully prepared to have them average 120 years of age, if anyone cared to count. The critical attitude gives one pause: A modern American playwright who composed a fantastic comedy, set in the present, featuring a Chorus of GAR members—would he be greeted with a flourish of actuarial tables?

70. *Pan's grotto:* A cave on the Akropolis containing a shrine to the god, outside the Citadel wall, which it adjoined on the northwest.

73. *That snake's a fabrication:* By inserting this speech (and the reply to it) I do not wish to make Lysistrata a religious skeptic, but to point out the joke. No one had ever seen the snake; even its most famous action, that of assisting Themistokles to persuade the Athenians to

abandon the city before the battle of Salamis, had been accomplished by its nonappearance.

page 78. *Kinesias:* A perfectly good Greek name, but in this context it evokes a pun on a common sexual application of the verb *kinein* "move."

87. *Only the table gets laid:* In the Greek, Kinesias compares his phallus to "Herakles at table"— a stock comedy bit wherein the glutton hero, raving with hunger, is systematically diddled of his dinner by his hosts.

91. *The Commissioner:* I maintain the Commissioner as Athens' representative in this scene (980-1013), not primarily because of the testimony of the manuscripts (shaky support at best), but from the logic and structure of the speeches themselves. Coulon assigns them to a *Prytanis,* or member of the Executive Board. In this he follows a whim of Wilamowitz, who took a hesitant suggestion by Van Leeuwen and exalted it into a new principal character in the play—one of the unhappiest changes ever made in an Aristophanic text. The caution of Van Leeuwen, who usually knew no fear as an editor, should have given anyone pause.

92. *a Spartan epistle:* Correctly, a *skytalê,* a tapered rod which was Sparta's contribution to cryptography. A strip of leather was wound about the rod, inscribed with the desired message, and unwound for transmission. A messenger then delivered the strip to the qualified recipient, who deciphered it by winding it around a rod uniform in size and shape with the first. Any interceptor found a meaningless string of letters.

94. *The most unnerving work of nature:* The ensuing reconciliation scene, with its surrogate sexuality, is one of the most curious in Aristophanes. It is not lyric; yet both its diction, oddly diffuse and redundant, and its meter, a paeonic variation on a common trochaic dialogue measure which paradoxically makes it much more

regular, seem to call for extensive choreography. I have tried to hedge my bet by stilting the English and employing an irregular scheme depending heavily on off-rhymes.

*page* 96. *CHORUS OF MEN:* Coulon, with most other modern editors, assigns the two strophes here (1043-57, 1058-71, pp. 96-97), plus the two which follow the subsequent scene (1189-1202, 1203-15, pp. 106-107), to the entire Chorus, which thereby demonstrates its new-found unity. This seems possible, but unarticulated; even in this play, antistrophic responsion does not necessarily indicate opposition. By paying attention to the matter of this Indian-giving, I have tried to indicate the appropriate diversity within unity: here, first Men (money), then Women (cooking); following Lysistrata's address, first Women (dress and ornament), then Men (grain). In any case, the manuscript indications, giving the first two strophes to the Women and the last two to the Men, appear impossible.

98. *Kinesias:* So I assign the leadership of the Athenians in this scene. Coulon follows Wilamowitz in allotting it to the latter's beloved "Prytanis." The manuscripts commit themselves no further than "Athenians," which is at least safe. It is definitely not the Commissioner.

99. *that self-appointed Purity League:* See Glossary, s.v. "Hermes."

103. *the Tyrant's days:* The reign of Hippias, expelled by the Athenians in 510 with the aid of Kleomenes and his Spartans, who defeated the tyrant's Thessalian allies.

105. *let's try Thessaly:* Puns on proper names, particularly geographical ones, rarely transfer well, and the following bits of sexual cartography will show. "Easy Mountain": an impossible pun on Mt. Oita, replacing the Greek's *Echinous*, a town in Thessaly whose name recalls *echinos*

"hedgehog"—slang for the female genitalia. "Maniac Gulf": for Maliac Gulf, with less dimension than the Greek's *Mêlia kolpon,* which puns both on bosom and pudendum. The "legs of Megara" are the walls that connected that city with her seaport, Nisaia.

*page* 108.   *to the door of the Akropolis:* This stage direction, and what follows it, attempt to make sense of a desperate situation in the manuscripts, whose chief accomplishment is to differentiate between Athenian and Spartan. In the passage 1216-46, I assign to the Commissioner those lines given by Coulon to the "Prytanis," and to Kinesias those he assigns to "an Athenian," with the following exceptions: the Koryphaios of Men receives 1216a ("Prytanis," Coulon) and 1221 ("Athenian," Coulon); the Commissioner receives 1226 ("Athenian," Coulon).

109.   *in Spartan:* This rendering of 1225 in dialect, and the reading of 1226 as an ironical question, is prompted by a notion of Wilamowitz', to whom an uncommon verb form seemed clear enough evidence of Spartan to warrant a native informant on stage 18 lines early. I am not sure of the validity of his perception, but it allows other solutions, such as the present one: Kinesias is awash with wine and international amity, and the Commissioner is amused.

111.   *LYSISTRATA:* Coulon, following Wilamowitz' ungallant suggestion, takes this speech from Lysistrata (1273-78) and gives it, plus the dubious line following the choral song (1295), to the "Prytanis"—thus crowning the play and turning a superfluous man into an unnecessary hero.

# Glossary

**ACHARNAI:** Largest of the rural demes of Attika, located about seven miles north of the city of Athens.

**ADONIS:** Mythical youth of marvelous beauty, beloved of Aphrodite, early cut off by a boar. His death was regularly bewailed by women of Greece and the East at summer festivals.

**AISCHYLOS, AESCHYLUS:** The great Athenian tragedian (525-456 B.C.).

**AJAX, AIAS:** Greek hero of the Trojan War, son of Telamon of Salamis.

**AKROPOLIS:** The citadel of Athens.

**AMAZONS:** The mythical race of warrior-women, said to have invaded Attika in heroic times to avenge the theft of their queen's sister, Antiope, by Theseus of Athens.

**AMYKLAI:** A Lakedaimonian town, traditional birthplace of Kastor (q.v.) and Pollux, site of a temple to Apollo.

**APHRODITE:** Goddess of beauty and sexual love.

**ARISTOGEITON:** Athenian hero who, with Harmodios, assassinated the tyrant Hipparchos in 514 and was put to death. With the expulsion of Hipparchos' brother Hippias four years later, the tyranny of the Peisistratids came to an end. Statues to Harmodios and Aristogeiton were erected in the Athenian Agora.

**ARTEMIS:** Goddess of the hunt and moon, sister of Apollo.

**ARTEMISIA:** Queen of Halikarnassos, who, as an ally of the Persian King Xerxes in his invasion of Greece, fought with particular distinction at the sea battle of Salamis in 480.

**ARTEMISION:** Site on the northern coast of Euboia, off which the Athenians defeated the Persians in a sea battle in 480.

**ATHENE, ATHENA:** Goddess of wisdom and war; patroness of Athens, and thus particularly associated with the Akropolis (q.v.).

BACCHOS: Dionysos, the god of vineyards, wine, and dramatic poetry, celebrated at Athens in a series of festivals, among them the Lenaia (January–February) and the City Dionysia (March–April).

BOIOTIA: A plentifully supplied state directly northeast of Attika, allied with Sparta during the Peloponnesian War.

CHARON: A minor deity in charge of ferrying the souls of the dead to Hades.

DEMETER: The Earth-Mother; goddess of grain, agriculture, and the harvest.

DEMOSTRATOS: A choleric Athenian demagogue, first to propose the disastrous Sicilian Expedition of 415-413.

EROS: God of sensual love, son of Aphrodite.

EURIPIDES: Athenian tragedian (480-406 B.C.), whose plays and private life furnished Aristophanes with endless material for ridicule. Euripides' determinedly ungallant representation of women (Phaidra in *Hippolytos*, for instance), alluded to in *Lysistrata*, becomes the basis for Aristophanes' next play, the *Thesmophoriazusae*.

EUROTAS: A river in Laconia, on which is located the city of Sparta.

HARMODIOS: Athenian hero; assassin, with Aristogeiton (q.v.), of the tyrant Hipparchos.

HEKATE: Goddess of the moon, night, childbirth, and the underworld.

HELEN: Daughter of Leda and Tyndaros, wife of Menelaos of Sparta. Her abduction by Paris of Troy furnished a *casus belli* for the Trojan War.

HERMES: God of messengers and thieves; in Athens in every doorway stood a statue of Hermes (i.e., a *herm*, usually a bust of the god surmounting an ithyphallic pillar), protector of the door and guardian against thieves—it takes one to know one. The wholesale mutilation of these statues by persons unknown, just before the sailing of the Sicilian expedition in 415, ted to the recall of Alkibiades—and thus, perhaps, to the loss of the expedition and ultimately of the war.

HIPPONAX: A satirical iambic poet of Ephesos (fl. 540

B.C.), noted for his limping meter and his touchy temper.

KARYSTIAN: From Karystos, a town in Euboia allied to Athens, whose male inhabitants enjoyed a seemingly deserved reputation for lechery.

KASTOR: Divinity, son of Leda and Tyndaros, or of Leda and Zeus; twin of Polydeukes (Pollux), with whom he constitutes the Dioskouroi. These twin gods were particularly honored by their native state of Sparta.

KIMON: One of Athens' greatest generals (died 449 B.C.); in the years following the Persian Wars, principal architect of the Athenian Empire—an activity abruptly interrupted by his ostracism in 461.

KLEISTHENES: A notorious homosexual; on that account, one of Aristophanes' favorite targets for at least twenty years.

KLEOMENES: Sixth-century king of Sparta, whose two Athenian expeditions had rather different results: The first, in 510, materially assisted in the expulsion of the tyrant Hippias; the second, in 508, failed to establish the power of the aristocratic party led by Isagoras.

KORINTH: Greek city allied to Sparta during the Peloponnesian War; situated on the strategic Isthmus of Korinth.

KYPROS: A large Greek island in the eastern Mediterranean, especially associated with the goddess Aphrodite, said to have stepped ashore there after her birth from the sea-foam.

LAKONIA: The southernmost state on the Greek mainland, Athens' principal opponent in the Peloponnesian War. Its capital city is Sparta.

LENAIA: An Athenian Dionysiac festival, celebrated in January–February.

LEONIDAS: Spartan king and general, who led his 300 troops against Xerxes' Persian army at Thermopylae in Thessaly (480).

MARATHON: A plain in eastern Attika; site of the famous battle (490 B.C.) in which the Athenian forces under Miltiades crushingly defeated the first Persian invasion of Hellas.

MEGARA: The Greek state immediately to the west of Attika; also, its capital city.

MELANION: A mighty hunter, evidently proverbial for his chastity. Probably not to be identified with Meilanion (Milanion), victorious suitor of the huntress Atalante.

MENELAOS: Legendary king of Sparta; husband of Helen (q.v.).

MESSENIA: The western half of Lakedaimon in the Peloponnese; in spite of revolutions, held by Sparta from ca. 730 B.C. until her defeat by Thebes at Leuktra in 371 B.C.

MIKON: A famous Athenian painter of murals, who flourished between the Persian and Peloponnesian Wars.

MILESIAN: From Miletos, a city in Karia in Asia Minor, which had broken off its alliance with Athens in mid-412, following the Sicilian disaster.

MYRONIDES: Athenian general in the period between the Wars; his best-known victory was over the Boiotians at Oinophyta (456).

PAN: Rural Arkadian god of the flocks and woodlands; his cult at Athens was instituted by way of thanks for his help to the Athenians at the battle of Marathon.

PEISANDROS: Engineer of the oligarchic revolt which overthrew the Athenian constitution in May 411 and set up the Council of Four Hundred.

PERIKLEIDAS: The ambassador sent by Sparta to beg Athenian aid in putting down the Messenian revolt of 464.

PHORMION: Athenian admiral, noted for his victory over the Korinthians at Naupaktos in 429.

POSEIDON: Brother of Zeus and god of the sea. As god of the sea, he girdles the earth and has it in his power, as Poseidon the Earthshaker, to cause earthquakes. In still another manifestation, he is Poseidon Hippios, patron god of horses and horsemen.

PYLOS: Town of the southwestern coast of Messenia whose capture by Athens, along with the neighboring island of Sphakteria, in 425-24, became a *cause célèbre* of the Peloponnesian War, and remained a thorn in Sparta's side until they retook it in 409.

SALAMIS: An island in the Saronic Gulf, between Megara

and Attika. Subject to Athens, it is divided from the shore by a narrow strait, site of the famous sea battle of 480 which saw the defeat of Xerxes' Persians by Themistokles' Athenians.

SAMOS: A large Aegean island lying off the coast of Ionia. At the beginning of 411, the effective headquarters of the Athenian forces, who had just aided a democratic revolution there. Other Athenians, especially Peisandros, were already fomenting an oligarchic counter-revolution.

SICILY: Scene of Athens' most disastrous undertaking during the war, the Sicilian Expedition of 415-413, which ended in the annihilation of the Athenian forces.

SKYTHIANS: Barbarians who lived in the region northeast of Thrace. Skythian archers were imported to Athens for use as police.

SPARTA: Capital city of Lakonia, principal opponent of Athens during the Peloponnesian War.

TAŸGETOS: A high mountain in central Lakedaimon that separates Lakonia from Messenia.

TELAMON: Legendary king of Salamis; father of Aias.

THASIAN: From Thasos, a volcanic island in the northern Aegean, celebrated for the dark, fragrant wine produced by its vineyards.

THEBES: The principal city of Boiotia; during the Peloponnesian War an ally of Sparta.

THEOGENES: An Athenian braggart, member of the war party.

THESSALY: A large district in northern Greece.

THRACE: The eastern half of the Balkan peninsula.

TIMON: The famous Athenian misanthrope, a contemporary of Aristophanes; a legend during his own lifetime.

ZAKYNTHOS: A large island in the Ionian Sea, south of Kephallenia and west of Elis; during the Peloponnesian War, an ally of Athens.

ZEUS: Chief god of the Olympian pantheon: son of Kronos, brother of Poseidon, father of Athene. As supreme ruler of the world, he is armed with thunder and lightning and creates storms and tempests.